BATTLES OF THE NIGHT

ARTEMIS LUPINE SERIES, BOOK FOUR

CATHERINE BANKS

Battles of the Night by Catherine Banks.

Copyright © 2019 Catherine Banks

Cover design by Covers by Juan.

Logo by Avery Banks.

Published by Turbo Kitten Industries.

www.CatherineBanks.com

Turbo Kitten Industries

PO Box 5012, Galt, CA 95632

RJ, thank you for all of your help, insight, assistance, guidance, and most of all, thank you for being my friend.

CR, thank you for your PA-ing help and all of the other things you help me with. You are amazing and I'm so lucky to have found someone like you to help me.

Special thanks to the following people
who backed my Kickstarter and helped
t these gorgeous books out into the world.

Amanda Jenkins	Louise Kendall
Anij Fallows	Matthea W. Ross
Arlene Medder	MelX
Brandy Robinson	Michelle Fritz
Ceciley Snook	Michelle Johnson
D. T. Brook	Michelle R. McFarlin
Davide B.	R.J. Blain
Deissy Hermunslie	Ran Frimark
Emily Suzanne Davis	Russell Nohelty
Emjrabbitwolf	Russell Ventimeglia
Fawn of the Woods	Stormie Harlan
Francesco Tehrani	Synergica
Gary Phillips	Taka Angevine
Helen Jensen	Tara Harrington
Jamie Forster	Zack Newcomb
Jeff Lewis	Amanda Haynes
ennifer & Jamie Wallace	Erin Hayes
Jennifer Laslie	Amber
Jon Tarbox	Emma
Ken Anderson	The Creative Fund
Kylie Corley	Rebecca Laffar-Smith

CHAPTER

ONE

KODA

I was over one thousand years old and felt as helpless as a newborn human.

There were few people whom I truly cared for. Ares was one I unashamedly loved. I stared at his lifeless body and hissed at my uselessness. Here I was, the most powerful vampire in the world, and I could do nothing, but wring my hands and pace.

I turned from Ares only to have my eyes come to rest on Artemis' body, which lay next to Ares' on top of the sarcophagus that should have been for Dmitri, had my father not made him an immortal vampire.

Artemis was small, beautiful, and enormously powerful. When I had first seen Ares and Artemis together, I was not sure what to make of the awkward, shy girl, but she soon proved that she was just as loyal and good hearted as the prophesied savior of the world should be. She was certainly capable of killing, but she had a good soul and most importantly she made Ares happy.

Ares and I had been through many battles and he had

1

saved my life numerous times. He had also put my life in danger just as many times, but no matter what we encountered, he never backed down and he constantly proved his loyalty to me. I wanted to prove my loyalty to him, to repay him, but I could do nothing.

"Any change?" asked a deep, growling voice from far away.

I walked out of the room and down the dark catacombs until I reached the stairs which led up into the cathedral where we were currently taking our refuge. A dark blue dragon's head snaked through the doorway of the cathedral and wound his way as close to the catacomb stairway as he could.

Draco Blu, leader of the dragons, had come an hour after Artemis' death demanding to know what had happened and seeking blood.

It was a good thing that Apollo, Artemis' twin brother and cause of her death, was locked deep within the catacombs or the dragon might have torn him apart and I did not think I would have been able to stop him. Draco Blu and Artemis had developed a friendship, which had shocked the entire world since the dragons had previously only kept to themselves. Knowing Artemis though, I felt that many would change their views after meeting her.

I met the dragon's eyes and shook my head.

He growled in frustration and asked, "How much longer can Hades hold him?"

Hades yelled, "Not much longer. I'm not strong enough to hold him more than another hour at most." Hades was a full-blooded Sidhe who had the unique power of being able to send people into Death's realm and bring them back…usually. He was currently the only thing keeping Ares alive, and the only link that would bring Ares back to the living realm.

Of course, that also depended on Death as well. If Death

decided that he wanted to keep Ares' soul with him, then there was nothing any of us could do.

Draco Blu pulled his head out of the cathedral and then returned only a few seconds later with one of his scales between his teeth.

I stared at it a moment before taking it from him and returning to the room where Hades was bent over Ares. I set the scale in Hades' hand and he gasped as the power flowed out of the scale and into him.

Hades blinked at it several times and then spoke to Draco Blu as I walked back to the stairway, "Why would you do this? Giving me some of your energy is an extreme gift, but you do not know me."

He simply said, "She is my friend."

I stared after the leader of the dragons.

In one thousand years, the dragons had not been friends with anyone. Now, the leader was giving his energy, his essence, to strangers to try to save a girl he viewed as his friend.

Times were definitely changing.

The dragon withdrew from the building and I returned to the room, leaned against the wall, and watched Ares again.

Koda walked into the room, still in his wolf form. Most werewolves were clean in their wolf forms because they switched forms a lot, but his fur was matted and looked oily and dingy. His eyes were glued to Artemis' body as he walked, as if she were the only thing in the room. The usually joyful and teasing man who always had a mohawk and crazy hair color had transformed with Artemis' death. As soon as Artemis had died, Koda shifted forms and refused to change back. I was slightly worried that he might go rogue, but more importantly, this was not like him.

He walked past me without even an acknowledgment and sat on the floor beside Artemis. He put his nose against her hand, inhaling her scent, and shuddered. He rubbed his face against her palm and then walked to Ares', repeating the movements. There were other wolves around, so he was not a lone wolf, but he had lost his brother Matt when Ares had had to execute him for being a traitor. To lose Artemis and Ares was too much for Koda to handle as a man, so he chose to stay a wolf. He jumped onto the stone, curled up at Artemis' feet, closed his eyes with a sigh, and fell asleep.

I left the room to find food before I lost control. Sidhe and wolves moved out of my way as I walked down the underground passageways. I realized after a moment that there was no food here, and I needed to teleport somewhere to find some. I closed my eyes and began to gather my magic to teleport to my favorite girl when a hand came to rest on my arm. "Victor," Dmitri whispered. "Take me with you please."

I opened my eyes and saw his pinched eyes and slightly elongated fangs and realized that I was failing as his leader. "I apologize. I should have remembered that you would need food as well."

I closed my eyes again and teleported us both to Las Vegas, not wanting to tell even Dmitri about my favored female. Vegas was one of the only areas that my father had not changed. For some reason he liked the bright lights and busyness. It was now home to hundreds of shapeshifters and vampires.

Dmitri smiled as we started walking and asked, "Are we going to get in a fight while we are here?"

I shrugged. "It depends on my father's minions. Most should know to steer clear of me and let me do as I want, but perhaps some will try to gain favoritism by attempting to capture me."

"Attempt would be the main word in that sentence," Dmitri said with a smile.

We walked down the sidewalks, passing by potion shops, clothing stores, strip clubs, and restaurants. The patrons of the town veered out of my path, which made me smile.

Or perhaps it was Dmitri they were avoiding. He was known as Fear and had been my father's right-hand assassin until I had freed him from my father's grasp.

With him beside me, I doubted we would have any trouble in this town, but one could always hope.

I stopped in front of a ten-story building with no markings on the front except for the address. "Here we are," I said with a smile as I pushed open the door.

A tall woman with exotic eyes sat behind a counter with a bored expression on her face. As soon as I entered, she stood up and smiled pleasantly at me. "Prince Victor. It has been too long since I have seen your handsome face."

"Alexandria, I have missed our meetings," I said with a bit of purr and sexual innuendo added along with some power in my voice.

Her body tightened in response to my power and she stepped around the counter to place her hands on my chest. She was slender and had thick blonde hair down to her butt. "What can I get for you?" she asked with heat in her eyes.

Dmitri rolled his eyes.

I smiled. "I need two donors for each of us. We are very thirsty."

She nodded and walked to an intercom, speaking in Russian and bending over just enough to make her skirt inch up her long legs. She motioned for us to follow her with a flick of her finger and tongue.

Dmitri shook his head at me, and I followed him without reading his thoughts, knowing well enough what he would be thinking.

Alexandria stopped at the first door and pushed it open. "Dmitri, you will feed here."

Dmitri stepped into the room and two beautiful Asian women stepped out from behind a curtain. "Hello, Dmitri," the identical twins said.

"Come, Victor," Alexandria prompted.

I waved to Dmitri and followed Alexandria to the room directly next to his. Alexandria pushed open the door and waved me in. "I hope you enjoy your meal."

"I appreciate your hospitality," I said and then picked her hand up and kissed the back of it.

She flushed and quickly turned away, retreating out the door she came through.

I opened the gate which I kept closed over my mind and focused on the two women sitting on the couch in front of me. I was strong, but even the strongest could fall prey to a trap and be killed. Women were often used as traps for men because we so often forget that women could be just as deadly. If men would only think about the lion and the fierceness of the lioness, the hunter of the pride, they might not forget to keep a knife nearby after lowering their defenses for a woman.

I never forgot.

The female vampire was just as capable at killing me as a male vampire. That was part of the enticement for me when mating with vampire women. They could turn from giving you sweet kisses to tearing open your throat with their fangs in a millisecond.

He's scary. I hope he isn't a messy eater.

Oh, he looks powerful. Look at those black eyes. I hope he chooses to feed from me first.

The humans who became cattle for vampires, were not usually the brightest, but I was surprised at the fierce look in the second's eyes and her desire to be fed from first.

I sat down on the couch between them and turned to the second girl. "I think I will start with you." I let my fangs extend fully, and she turned her neck to the side, presenting me with a perfect angle to puncture her neck. It was nice to have such pretty food sometimes.

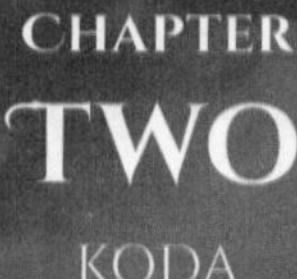

CHAPTER
TWO

KODA

Miss Alpha.

    Miss Alpha female.

Want pack back.

Lonely. So lonely without.

Need to eat. Need to rip into something's stomach. Mm, fresh liver. Blood smells good in forest. Blood. Want blood.

No. Alpha and Alpha female not happy if I kill.

Want her back. Want her warmth back.

Whine.

Pain. Hurts. Need her back.

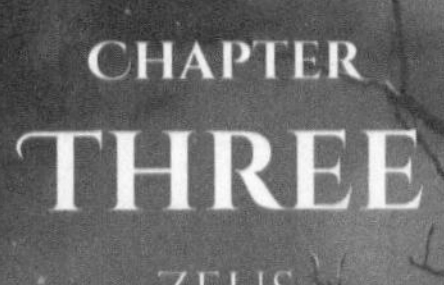

This battle had not gone anything like I had thought it would. My youngest son, one of the strongest of the Sidhe, lay on top of someone else's grave, cold to the touch. My other son lay on another grave in Death's realm trying to retrieve his mate's soul. Poor Artemis, who had been through more than one being should be forced to go through was dead just like Achilles, her death caused by their bond which he had created to save her.

Hera, my wife, still sat beside Achilles, holding his hand as if she expected him to awaken and sit up from a dream. How I wished this was all a dream! In one day, I could lose both of my sons and my daughter-in-law. It was too much for a parent to bear.

I should have been strong enough to take out Maurice myself, but the sad fact was that I had lost most of my magic when I had battled Goliath, the former Werewolf King and Beatrice's father, and he had torn one of the wings from my back. My wing had regenerated, but my magic was a quarter of what it had been.

None of this was right. Achilles was supposed to live thousands of years after I died. He was supposed to rule over the Sidhe with Artemis at his side.

Achilles had always been a loving and caring child. I had been proud to see him carry that on into his adulthood. He had been shaping up to become an amazing king.

Despite all of the issues surrounding Ares, Achilles had always loved and looked up to him.

Hera and I had caused the rift between the brothers. I had caused my sons so much pain during their lives.

I had failed as a father, I already knew that.

My two sons had finally started to mend the rift between them and now this had happened.

Now, I had failed as a king.

Tears slipped silently down my face and I covered my eyes with my hands.

It should have been my son mourning me. Not me mourning my son. I shouldn't have had to listen to my wife mourn our boy.

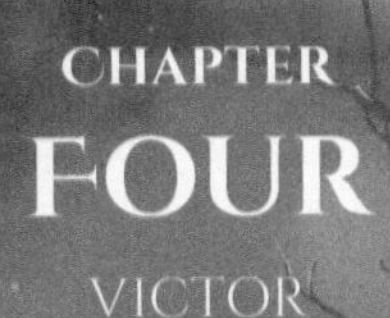

I sat dozing in one of the chairs in the room where Ares' and Artemis' bodies lay. I had fed and returned quickly, not wanting to miss Ares' return. Two more hours had passed, and I was quickly losing my ability to stay awake.

Hades gasped. "Victor! He's coming back."

I was alert and instantly on my feet. Koda climbed down from where he had been lying at Artemis' feet and stood beside me, facing Ares' body. We stood side by side, both rigid in anticipation and worry. Hades closed his eyes in concentration and grunted just as Ares took a gasping breath and sat up.

His eyes met mine, and he whispered, "Find me a steak."

Koda whined and wagged his tail, and Ares frowned down at him. "You thought I wouldn't come back?"

Koda flattened his ears to his head and crawled on his belly towards Ares.

Ares set his hand on Koda's head and smiled. "I would not leave you alone, Brother." Ares turned and looked at Artemis' still body a moment before looking at me with a small smile. "She's pregnant."

I stared at him a moment before comprehending what he had said. Had he forgotten what had happened? Had he dreamed instead of going to Death's realm?

"Ares, she's not alive," I whispered to him.

He waved his hand dismissively at me. "She will be in a little bit. I just need to take her outside so she can be resurrected."

"Resurrected?" I asked.

He stood slowly, testing his body, and whispered, "Death agreed to let me have both of their souls back."

That was not uncommon. Many had traveled to Death and had a life returned, but all was done at an extreme cost. "What price was asked of you?"

Ares walked to Artemis and stroked her hair, looking at her with so much love that it felt like an invasion to even witness him next to her.

"Ares, what price was asked of you?" I asked again.

He picked her body up in his arms and cradled her against his chest. "Come, their souls need to return to her body."

I grabbed his arm and his lips pulled back over his teeth as he snarled at me.

"Ares, tell me," I insisted.

He smiled. "None, because I demanded their souls back as the God of War." His smile became darker and he said, "And I smelled Death's fear."

I stared at him in astonishment. "You think Death will leave it at that?"

Ares smiled brightly and said, "I will deal with that when the time comes. For now, let's go enjoy the moonlight and the last bit of quiet before Artemis wakes up."

The joy on his face, the absurdity of everything that was happening, it broke the shell of worry surrounding me.

With a chuckle, I followed him out of the room.

13

FIVE

I hated Artemis feeling, smelling, and looking so dead in my arms. I hurried from the room, out of the catacombs, through the cathedral, and out to the open grassy area outside.

My mind was still reeling from the conversation with Death, but that was something I didn't have to worry about for a long time. For now, I had only to focus on Artemis and our child inside of her.

I laid her down on the grass and Draco Blu approached.

His huge body towered over us both, his scales gleaming in the fading sunlight, and yet his eyes were soft as he looked down at my mate. "What happened?" he asked.

I smiled at him. "I came to an agreement with Death. Artemis will be alive again as soon as the moon's and the stars' lights shine upon her face."

Draco Blu lowered his head until it was level with mine, his eye staring straight into my own, and whispered, "I will help you with the price, if you need it. I know Death asks a lot of those souls it releases."

It was the greatest offering any could give, especially considering I had almost killed off his entire race.

I bowed my head and whispered, "I am honored at your offer."

He snorted softly, dual rings of smoke rising from his nostrils. "I offer only because she is my friend and valuable to all. You alone should not be forced to carry the burden just because she is your match."

I had known he was not offering for me, but I found it amusing that he felt the need to point it out.

I was barely able to keep the smirk off my face. "Luckily, no price was required," I whispered to him.

He snorted again, this time in disbelief, and I smiled, enjoying the shock on his face.

The sun began to set and a crowd started to gather. Koda, still in wolf form, kept everyone back to give us room.

I kissed Artemis gently on the lips and moved a little ways away from her.

Zeus made his way through the crowd and sat down next to me on the grass. His face was drawn, his eyes pinched, and for the first time in his life he had bags beneath his eyes. Achilles' death was taking a toll on my father. He most likely had found some way to blame himself, as he often took the blame for things not his doing. And, he was likely mourning Artemis as well. He had grown attached to her rather quickly.

"Will you help protect those gathered?" I asked him.

He nodded. "I will shield everyone else, but you must shield yourself from her when she wakes up."

The return of a soul to a being of power was often catastrophic for those nearby. Artemis' return was bound to be cataclysmic due to her amount of power. Hopefully, it wouldn't be nearly as bad as when she had broken the barrier and regained her memories since we only had four dragons with us this time.

I nodded at Zeus and prepared a shield around myself. Koda stepped out into the circle of people and Zeus raised a shield of power around all of us. I raised my shield and spread it to cover Zeus. Draco Blu and the other dragons that had come also put shields around us, singing to invoke their magic.

I only hoped it was enough.

The sun set and everyone became silent in anticipation. The moon rose and the stars glittered brightly, yet Artemis lay still.

I started to move, but Draco Blu whispered, "Look."

The moon's light flared, and a beam like a spotlight high-lighted Artemis. The stars flared brighter and they formed a unified beam down on her. Her body twitched once and lay still again. Her chest rose and fell with breath, but I dared not move. The stars and moon shone brighter than our eyes could handle, forcing us to close them. Power greater than any I had ever encountered before pressed down upon us, and then Artemis began to scream.

I forced open my eyes, squinting against the light, but needing to see what was happening to my mate.

Artemis floated in the air, her wings extended, her skin the source of the shining. Her eyes were orbs of white and her stomach glowed blue. She stopped screaming and sighed as the power left her in a wave of fire that burned through our shields and knocked those nearby to the ground.

I crawled to her body, ignoring the pain and the still sizzling grass.

She lay on the ground, sleeping peacefully.

After pressing my ear to her stomach and hearing Artemis'

heartbeat as well as our child's, I cried. The sorrow I felt at her death, the pain from carrying her lifeless body from the battlefield, the hurt knowing she loved Achilles, and the grief I felt at losing Achilles. I released all the pain and wept at the return of my soul mate, my *passt genau,* while those around me cheered.

My body felt stiff and uncomfortable, but I knew I had to get up because something was happening. I could feel Ares touching me, but people around us were shouting and dragons were roaring so loudly that I could not hear him.

I opened my eyes and whispered, "What's going on?"

The ground around us was burned and some bits still smoking. It looked like all of our allies were gathered around us, most sitting on the ground with huge smiles on their faces. Some were even crying.

Ares lifted his face from my stomach but the wetness of his tears remained. "Are you hungry?" he asked softly.

Of all of the things I had expected him to say, that was not one of them.

I nodded and started to stand, but he picked me up in his arms and cradled me against his chest. I relaxed against his familiar touch and the wonderful warmth of him, letting his body heat warm my chilled body.

He walked past a crowd of smiling people who all looked at me with awe.

What had happened while I was asleep?

Ares set me down on a padded pew in a large, empty cathedral and a young girl brought a bowl of soup to me.

I sipped the soup, and then my hunger took over and I gulped it down in eager swallows.

Ares took the empty bowl and handed me a plate with two slabs of meat on it. He ate a third slab of meat. I ate my meat just as quickly as I had eaten the soup, and more food was brought to me. After thirty minutes of stuffing my face, I was finally full.

I leaned back against the pew and patted the spot beside me.

Ares sat down next to me and hugged me tightly, wrapping his entire body around mine.

I gently rubbed his back. "Ares, what has happened? Why were you crying when I woke up?"

He pulled away and ran the back of his hand gently down my face, caressing me and smiling tenderly. "What is the last thing you remember?"

I tried to think, but the last thing I remembered was the fight and…

I gasped. "Achilles! Oh no, Ares please tell me that he is alright." My heart constricted, and I knew the truth without Ares having to say it.

Ares took my hands in his and whispered, "During the battle, he was stabbed in the heart and instantly died. You both fell and because you were bound to him. You…" He choked on his words and couldn't finish the statement.

"I died," I whispered.

Ares swallowed, trying to keep his emotions at bay. "Yes."

I shivered and climbed into his lap, hiding my face against

his chest. I couldn't believe that I had died. "How did I come back?"

"I demanded your life back from Death," Ares said in a serious tone.

I looked up at him. "You did what?"

He smiled. "With Hades' help, I entered Death's realm and demanded your life back." He put a hand on my stomach and whispered, "As well as the life of our baby."

I stared at his hand sitting on my flat stomach and said, "You're joking."

He shook his head. "You're pregnant. That is why you were throwing up and why you were so moody."

I was pregnant. I stared in disbelief at my stomach a moment before closing my eyes and focusing on my body. There, in the center of my stomach, I felt the power of another being, small, but still very much there. I was pregnant.

"I'm going to be a mom," I whispered. I looked at Ares' happy face and smiled. "We're going to have a baby."

He kissed my lips and I melted against him, kissing him back as though it had been years since we had last kissed. His lips burned mine, and I shivered from the difference in our body heat. How long would it take my formerly dead body to heat back up?

After a few minutes, he pulled away with a somber expression on his face. "I am sorry that our news is tainted. I would have preferred we were able to fully enjoy this."

I stood up and stretched my stiff body. How long had I been dead? I was not sure what to expect, but I would have thought that my body would be stiffer than it was. "I agree, but we have had our moment of joy. Perhaps it is time to deal with our grief and begin grieving," I said.

Until I saw Achilles' body, I could not believe that it was true that he was dead. It had to be a cruel joke. He had been so alive. I remembered his fierce face during battle and the compassion he showed me when we were alone. I could not believe he was dead now. It did not seem possible.

Ares linked his fingers with mine and led me down a stairway into dark catacombs.

Koda bounded inside in his wolf form and knocked me to the ground, licking my face.

I laughed and pushed his face away, wiping the slobber off. I pet Koda's head and asked, "Why are you in wolf form?"

"Because he thought you and I were gone and not going to return," Ares answered for him with a bit of anger in his tone.

I tapped Koda's nose in a playful discipline. "You should know better than that."

Koda grunted and then looked up at Ares. Apparently, he had been in wolf form too long and could not change back on his own.

Ares grabbed Koda by his scruff and growled into his face as he used his power to force the change.

Koda whined and then moaned as he shifted into his human form.

Ares released Koda and grabbed my hand again. "Eat something and then wait for us to summon you."

"Yes, Alpha," Koda said softly as he panted, naked on the floor.

Ares led me down a hallway to another room which had five Sidhe males guarding it. The guards gaped at me for a moment before stepping aside and opening the doors. Apparently, they weren't used to seeing people back from the dead.

The room was cold and empty except for Hera, Zeus, and a table with Achilles' body lying on top of it.

I pulled out of Ares' hand and walked to Achilles, feeling like I was in a dream. He looked so much more handsome than I remembered him being and so at peace. I reached out slowly and rested my hand against his cheek. Instantly tears rolled down my face as the warmth that usually radiated from him was gone.

He felt cold, like stone.

I sobbed and cried as I held his lifeless hand in mine. He had died protecting me. It was cruel that I was alive again while he was not. He had watched me and loved me since I was a child. He had bound me to him to protect me and had endured so much for me. I had not been able to spend enough time with him. I loved him, but not as he had deserved to be loved and he had not been allowed to love me as he had wanted.

Ares wrapped his arms around me to comfort me, but that only increased my sorrow.

If Achilles had found me first, what would things have been like? Would I be carrying Achilles' child now instead of Ares'? Would I have been fighting this war or would we have been somewhere safe, away from the battle which took both of our lives?

The sounds of sorrow poured from my mouth, but all I could see or hear were memories of Achilles and the awful understanding that I would never experience them again. I would never see his smile. I would never see his vines glow or his power open when I touched him. I would never see his wings spread and watch him take flight. I would never again hear his voice in my head. I would never again hear him speak Latin to me.

He was gone before I had ever gotten to have him. It wasn't fair!

I felt my body begin to heat up, but I did not care about the repercussions. Ares said something to me, but I pushed him away from me. I climbed onto Achilles, straddling his body, and called my power. I called to all of the plants and trees. I called to the moon and the stars. I called to the goddess or god or whatever being created us. I called them all to me and pulled the power into my hands.

Ares was yelling at me, but I ignored him.

I raised my hands and prepared to pour the power into Achilles to try to resurrect him when Zeus touched my arms and whispered, "You must not mourn the times you did not have, but remember and cherish the times you did have."

"I can raise him. I can bring him back," I said in a voice that sounded strange even to me.

Zeus shook his head. "You could raise him from the dead, but he would not be the Achilles you loved or the son I loved. His soul has been gone for too long. Besides, you would not be bound to him anymore."

"I can bring him back," I insisted.

Zeus gently grabbed my arms and whispered, "He died to save you because he loved you. Do not let his sacrifice be for nothing. Release the power before it kills you and the child you carry. Let his soul rest."

I screamed in grief, pain, and loss and released the powers.

Zeus caught me before I fell and whispered, "Remember, Artemis. That is all he would want. He would only want you to remember him."

Ares reached for me, but I jerked away from him. I could not let him comfort me over Achilles' death. It was not fair to Achilles.

I used some of my power and teleported to Ares' house in

Russia, knowing that no one would be there and that it was one place Ares would not look for me.

The living room looked just like I remembered it and thankfully there was no one inside. I collapsed onto the couch and let the tears flow again. Achilles was dead, and I had not been able to help him. If only I had been faster. If only I had not been a burden to him. I had been pushing him away and now he was gone forever. All I wanted was one touch. Just one whispered word. I wanted to hear his voice and feel his skin touch mine. I tried to stop crying, but could not.

Hours passed as my sorrow poured out of my body in cries, sobs, and screams of agony. I was tired of losing people whom I loved.

The day turned into night and the river of tears turned into a trickle. I knew I should eat, but the grief I felt over losing Achilles was too much to bear. I buried my face into the pillows and let more of my grief lose by way of tears and uncontrollable sobs.

DAY TWO

The pain became so unbearable that my wolf took over, and I shifted forms despite the small fear I had that I would not be able to change back again. My wolf felt as sad as I did and instead of cries and sobs, I released my pain in heartbroken howls.

Why hadn't I been able to protect him?

I missed him.

DAY THREE

Part of us missed our mate, but part of us was too sad about losing our other non-wolf, sort of mate. He had been nice and warm and smelled great. We missed his scent.

Pain made me whine and then the howls tore out of our throat again.

DAY FOUR

My stomach hurt, and I needed food to feed the baby I was growing. Despite the weakness that I felt, I shifted to my human form and opened the door, walking down the stairs until we reached the bottom floor, and opened that door.

Cold air pierced my skin and I welcomed its pain. This pain meant that I was alive. It was good to know that I was alive, even if Achilles was not. I shifted forms again and raced towards the nearest restaurant, searching for scraps in the dumpster, too tired to hunt anything formidable. Luckily, I was able to find meat scraps outside of a butcher's shop, and I ate what I could find, fighting off rats and stray animals.

The wind whistled down the alley and a bright blue light shone at the end.

Achilles!

I ran down the alley, yipping in excitement as I chased after him. I knew he couldn't be dead! I ran as fast as I could and pounced at the light, slamming into a building. I shook myself and looked up, stunned to see a blue lantern affixed to the building. No Achilles.

I whined as pain filled my chest and then growled at my stupidity. He was gone, and I had to deal with that fact. No matter how much I wanted him, he was never coming back again.

I ambled to the house, shivering in the cold as snow landed on my back and muzzle. I shifted forms to open and close the doors and then crawled into the bed which had a very warm blanket on it and fell asleep replaying the memories which Achilles had shared with me when he had bound us together.

DAY FIVE

The pain was gone and replaced by a vast numbness. I sat very still and became aware that I was not handling my grieving process very well. I growled in frustration and shook my head. I missed Achilles, but I could not be so immature and inconsiderate. Ares had saved me and I had abandoned him. I needed to finish my grieving and return to Ares.

The memory of Achilles' dead body flashed before me, and I curled up into a ball on the bed.

Tomorrow, I would return to Ares.

DAY SIX

At some point I had moved from the bed to the couch, only to be awoken by the scent of vampires drawing near me. I held my position and kept my eyes closed, waiting for them to get closer.

"We heard rumors of a wolf howling and assumed it might be someone from your pack," one of the vampires said sounding very arrogant for only seeing me and not having captured me yet. He still had to capture me before he could sound that smug.

I opened my eyes and was shocked to find myself surrounded by vampires.

Okay, maybe his smugness wasn't so hard to believe.

I growled and sprung from my sleeping position up into a crouch, ready to attack and shift if need be. "What do you want?" I asked as I assessed my options.

There were twelve vampires in the room in a circle around me and several more out in the hallway, though I had no idea how many since they were not in view so I could have been vastly outnumbered. I could use my fire, but then I would end up burning down Ares' house, which I was sure would not be okay with him. He would forgive me, but I did not want to burn down the pretty building. If I'd had any energy, I could have teleported.

"We want you to come with us peacefully to see the King," he said pleasantly.

I could use my sunlight magic, but I had to be sure to get every vampire here, otherwise if I missed one, he would go to Maurice and spill my secret.

Wait.

If I was taken to Maurice, then I could kill him there! Even if they bound me and blindfolded me, I could still use my sunlight magic. It could be a quick end to this entire battle! No one else would die needlessly.

"Will you promise not to hurt me?" I asked softly, trying to feign a little bit of fear. "I am pregnant."

The vampires all blinked at my news, but the leader nodded. "I swear we will not cause you or your unborn child harm if you come with us willingly."

I stood up and smoothed down my clothes. "Okay. Let's go."

My answer seemed to surprise them more than my announcement of being pregnant, but after a second of gawking, two of the vampires took me by my arms and led me out of the house. A third vampire came and tied my hands behind my back as we walked. I had wondered what measures they would take to secure me at least in some way. Not that I couldn't break out of the ropes easily, but I let them have their imaginary safety. Now that we were out, I could finally count the total number of vampires and was surprised and a little prideful that they had sent thirty vampires after me. Not that one hundred could have captured me if I had not wanted to be captured, but it still meant that they thought I was a threat.

The vampires whispered to each other for a couple of minutes and then the leader asked, "If we allow you to fly, will you try to escape?"

Were they really giving me this option? In normal circumstances, I would have agreed and then immediately escaped. "I will not try to escape. I want this war over before anyone else I love dies."

He sensed my truthfulness and must have seen the pain on my face at the mentioning of my loved ones dying. "Very well.

We will tie your hands in front of you to allow you to fly beside us. If you try to escape, I will kill you."

I kept a grim look on my face and said, "I understand".

One of the other vampires untied my hands from behind my back and retied them in front. Once the vampire was sure the ropes were tight, he nodded at the leader.

"Let's go," he said. As one the vampires transformed into bats. It happened in the blink of an eye and was quite impressive. I took a deep breath and gathered my magic, urging it into my back and forcing my wings out. The cool night air swirled around me and I drank it in in big gulps. I had stayed cooped up in the house too long and denied myself the outdoors.

The vampires circled overhead as they waited for me to make a move. I could fly away and return to Ares. Or I could follow the vampires and confront Maurice. Part of me wanted to escape and return to safety, but a larger part of me knew I needed to face Maurice and end this war.

I flapped my wings and joined them in the sky. One of the bats squeaked and then they all took off. I flew along beside them, trying not to think about my impending fight and possible death. I had to live or Ares' journey into Death's realm would have been for nothing.

We flew for what felt like an hour before finally seeing the Eiffel Tower. Why had they left the Eiffel Tower intact? Memories of my first visit to the city made me cringe and miss Ares. I had put my mate through more than any living being should have had to endure. I had to end this war so that we could begin a normal life together. A life that did not involve me or anyone else dying until we were very very old. I laughed at the thought of how old Ares already was. I wasn't exactly a spring chicken either. Where had the time gone? I was over one hundred years old and having my first child. That would have been something I would have laughed at before I had met Ares. Before I had met Ares, I had thought it was crazy for a woman over forty to have a child. Things had changed so much.

The vampires switched forms, landing lightly on their feet in front of a palace. "Where are we?" I asked.

"This used to be the king and queen's when they were ruling here," the leader said.

How fitting that the vampire who thought he was supreme ruler would live in a palace that used to be a monarch's. I followed them inside the building and was shocked to find it full of vampires. Several hissed at me or bared their fangs when they caught sight of me. I showed them my teeth and growled. I may have surrendered, but I was not afraid of them and would protect myself if they attacked me.

A man who was completely covered by a large black robe stopped our group. "What's your business?"

"We are bringing Artemis Lupine to King Maurice. She surrendered herself to us."

I took long draws of air in through my nose trying to catch the robed man's scent, but I could not find it. Who was he? Better yet, *what* was he?

"I will accompany you," the robed man said and walked to the back of the group of vampires escorting me.

"Who was that?" I asked, hoping to receive an answer, but sadly I only received silence from them.

We continued forward, walking to a large ballroom where Maurice sat on a throne watching vampires dancing and talking. The vampire women were all dressed in extravagant gowns and wore hundreds of diamonds while the vampire men were dressed in tuxedos. As we entered the room his eyes found mine and a smile spread across his lips. "Welcome, Artemis Lupine, Queen of the Werewolves and Princess of the Sidhe. It has been too long since we last met."

I played polite dignitary and curtsied to him. "Thank you for your warm greeting, King Maurice. Your new place is lovely."

"Thank you. I enjoy it here."

"May I have my hands untied? I am with child and surely no threat to someone as powerful as you."

"With child? Is it the Sidhe's or the werewolf's?" he asked as he motioned at the robed man to untie my hands.

"It is Ares' child," I said as I fought to keep the pain from my voice and hold in the whine that wanted to escape.

The robed man stopped in front of me and I tried to catch a glimpse of his face, but the robe hung too far over. I took in a deep breath and still could not smell him. He cut the ropes with a dagger, being sure not to let his skin touch mine and then stepped away from me.

I rubbed my wrists and smiled at Maurice. "Thank you."

"Come, sit beside me, Artemis, and rest your feet. I hear women's ankles swell during pregnancy."

I walked towards him and wondered what he was up to. How could he be so calm and so at ease with me approaching him? I sat down and looked at the large group of vampires inside the room and the robed man. What were my best options for killing them all?

"I bet you are wondering about my plan to defeat the little rebellion your group is involved with, aren't you?" Maurice asked.

I did not say anything because I figured he was not looking for me to speak, only for me to listen to his *wonderful* plan.

"At this moment my vampires are moving to strategic

points around the world. They will sit in hiding, waiting until they are given the word from me to attack. Once your group comes and challenges me, the deployed vampires will attack, killing those that have been left behind. All of those submissive wolves, Sidhe, and elves won't stand a chance against my vampires."

He was right that he would kill hundreds if not thousands, but now that I knew his plan, there was no way he would get away with it. Or did he think it did not matter? Did he want to try to scare me into stopping the assault on him?

Did he not view me as a threat? Did he really think that I was captured and now his prisoner? My anger boiled over and I let my magic fill me. I pictured Achilles' dead body and let it fuel my anger until my body was shining too brightly for any to keep their eyes open. I formed sunlight around me in a circle and sent it outwards in an ever-expanding wave, killing the vampires in the room before they could even draw in a breath to scream.

I looked at the throne and felt terror run through my body in a wild chill. Maurice sat calmly on the throne, examining his fingernails as the sunlight drenched him. "Why isn't it affecting you?" I asked as I backed away from him, stirring up the ashes of the dead vampires on the ground.

"I am the original vampire, the first," he said as he stood up and let his fangs fully extend. "Did you really think that a little thing like sunlight would kill me?"

I gathered my magic and tried to teleport but doing so made me dizzy and nauseous. Was it from being pregnant? Or was it because I had not eaten in two days? I had to teleport. I had to escape! I tried again but could not move anywhere.

The robed man stepped forward and removed his hood. He was tall, ugly with a much too large nose for his face and had an evilly confident smile. "You cannot teleport so long as I, Merlin, the greatest sorcerer in the world, am alive."

I focused on my wolf, transformed into a half-shift and said, "Then I shall fix that issue."

I charged at him, but a sword appeared in his hand and he swung it at me, barely missing my stomach. I jumped backwards and formed a sword from my body. I would not let him win. I charged at him again, blocking his sword with mine and trying my hardest to disarm him. He parried each strike I made and did it with a smug smile. I formed claws from my left hand and sliced at his face, hoping to rip that smile off, but he dodged, and Maurice stepped between us.

I swung my sword at Maurice's chest, but he turned his torso into mist and my blade went through him. "You cannot win, Artemis. I do commend you for your effort, but you are no match for me."

I screamed at him and formed fire, the only other thing that scared a vampire as much as sunlight. He turned into mist and flew quickly across the ballroom, out of the fire's path. Before I could gather enough magic to engulf the entire room in fire, Merlin attacked me, using a magic staff in addition to his sword. Something about the staff made my hackles rise. I wasn't positive what was wrong with it, but I knew I needed to keep it from touching me. He struck at me with the staff and I recoiled from it and the smell of death which permeated from it.

I focused on my magic and the plants outside of the building we were in, drawing all of the magic to me while still battling Merlin. Maurice appeared behind me and I released my magic in the form of a fire circle. As I had expected, Maurice turned to mist and flew up into the ceiling. I formed a ball around myself with the fire and grunted as I thrust the fire out, adding additional fire to it as it moved and making it expand. Maurice cursed and I smiled, knowing I had trapped him. The fire expanded until it engulfed the entire room, setting Merlin on fire and catching part of Maurice on fire just before he slipped out one of the doors.

I wanted to chase after him, but I had pressed my luck too far as it was. I teleported back to Ares' Russian house and found Ares and Victor sitting in the living room on the couch. How the hell had they found me?

"You want to explain to me why you let vampires capture you and take you to see Maurice?" Ares asked calmly with his arms crossed over his chest.

"I had a plan. It was a great plan. It would have worked too if that stupid Merlin had not been there." I said as I took deep breaths to slow my racing heart.

"You thought you could kill Maurice with sunlight and end the war," Victor said. "And no, I did not read your mind. I just know you."

"That is very like her," Ares grumbled. "Risking herself to try to end this battle. Although I had hoped she would not do those types of things now that she is pregnant."

"They swore they would not harm me or the child while they took me to Maurice," I said irritated. "It would have worked if he had not been immune to sunlight. I almost got him with fire, but he misted out a door."

Ares shook his head sadly. "And here I thought you would be in need of consoling, not saving."

"I was grieving and then they showed up," I whispered, feeling insecure about not still grieving for Achilles.

"One has little time to grieve in times of war," Victor said, reading my thoughts.

"How did you find me?" I asked without moving closer to

them. Part of me wanted to run to Ares, but part of me felt like it would be a betrayal to Achilles whom I *was* still grieving for.

"We thought of all of the places that we would normally think you would go to and then immediately crossed those off of our list. Then we made a list of all of the places that you knew of and picked the few that we thought you would go to and think we would not think of going," Ares said. "It's simple Artemis logic really."

"Simple," Victor said with a chuckle.

I glared at Victor and then turned away, looking out the window and trying to sort through my feelings. Once I was calm again, I turned around and they both gave me the look. "What?" I asked.

"You cannot go off by yourself and try to take out the King of the Vampires," Ares said sternly, as though he were lecturing a teenager. "You have duties, responsibilities and a child to think about now."

I resisted the urge to answer with "Yes, Father" and simply bit my tongue. Of course, Victor read my mind and laughed, turning away from us and heading into the kitchen.

"I was thinking about my responsibilities. I *almost* killed him," I answered as I plopped down on the couch. Now that I was not in a fight, a headache had decided to rear its awful head and begin torturing me.

"What's wrong?" Ares asked and then sat down beside me, moving my hands away from my face.

"I just have a headache," I whispered, wishing for once that his touch was not so soothing. Would the pain of Achilles' loss ever leave? Or would I always feel this regret and pain when Ares touched me? Why did I feel like I was cheating?

"It will get better," Ares whispered as he pulled his hands away.

I was not so sure about that. The only way I could see it getting better was to forget him and I would *never* do that.

"We have had many die around us, Artemis. Trust us. In time it will be bearable," Victor said as he poured himself a glass of whiskey from the cupboard in the kitchen.

"Are you here to bring me back?" I asked Ares. How could I face Hera and Zeus? Would they ever be able to forgive me for causing their son's death? Was Ares upset at me for causing his brother's death? They had only recently become close and now his brother was gone forever.

"We mainly came to ensure that you were not getting into any trouble," Ares said.

"Which of course you were," Victor said as he walked to the large reclining chair and sat in it with his glass of whiskey.

I ignored his comment and asked, "When do we have to go back?"

Ares shrugged. "Probably soon since Maurice will be angry that you killed a lot of his vampires, the warlock, and that you almost killed him."

"There are probably fifty or more vampires headed our way as we speak," Victor said with a strange light in his eyes.

"So, are we going to stay and kill them or are we leaving?" I asked. It was strange that Ares wasn't whisking me away to safety knowing that we would soon be attacked. It was especially strange since I was pregnant.

"We will be leaving in a moment," Victor said sadly, "Before the vampires arrive."

"You sound like you want to get in a fight," I said.

Victor smiled. "I do."

"We all do," Ares said with a growl.

My headache intensified, causing me to double over in pain and hang my head between my legs. "Can we go now?" I asked.

"Yes," Ares said, standing up and then picking me up from the couch.

"Can you teleport us?" I asked Victor. "I am in too much pain to do it."

"Of course," he said as he stood up and walked to us. He chugged the rest of his whiskey and then set a hand on each of our shoulders. "Just throw up on Ares if you need to."

The world twisted around us and then we were in the underground of the cathedral again, inside the room with Achilles' body. "Why are we here?" I asked, swallowing back the tears that tried to surface.

"Because I want to speak to you," Zeus said from behind us. Ares turned around so that we were facing Zeus who was sitting on a stone bench.

I felt more nervous facing him than I had anyone else. Hera popped into the room using her teleportation and sat down on the bench beside Zeus. "Did I miss anything?"

Zeus shook his head. "They just arrived."

"Good," she said.

"What's up?" I asked nervously.

"Victor, would you please leave us?" Zeus asked.

Victor bowed to Zeus and Hera and said, "Of course." He winked at me and then disappeared in a whirl of mist.

"How are you feeling?" Zeus asked me as he and Hera just looked at me.

What was going on? Why had they called me here? "I'm okay. I have a bit of a headache, but I'm sure that will be cured when I eat some food."

"When was the last time you ate?" Hera asked.

"Two days ago," I whispered, wishing Ares was not there to hear.

"Two days?" Ares hissed, setting me down on my feet. "Why haven't you eaten in two days?"

"Ares," Zeus reprimanded, "Calm down."

"You cannot starve yourself. You have a baby inside of you now and you must take care of it above yourself," Ares said with a rumble in his voice. "I will leave her here with you and get food for her."

"Ares, don't leave me," I begged him.

"Zeus will protect you if you get yourself into trouble, yet again, while I am gone," Ares said and then walked out of the room.

I stared at the door in shock. He rarely got angry with me. Was it because of the baby? Or was this also because of Achilles?

"Are you able to fully use your magic and fully change?" Hera asked.

I sighed. "Yes."

"Do you have any side effects that you have noticed?" She asked.

I frowned. "No."

"Good. You are one of the few that have returned from Death's realm so we wanted to make sure that you were doing alright," Zeus said.

I cringed, knowing that if it were up to them that they would have wanted Achilles back as well.

"We brought you here to check on you and to tell you that we do not blame you," Hera said.

I trembled to my core. "What?"

"We do not blame you for our son's death," Zeus said, glancing quickly at Achilles' body before looking back at me.

I didn't know what to say. The only thing I could think to do was apologize to them and they did not seem like they wanted my apology, so I just stood there.

I blamed myself. How could they not blame me?

Zeus came over to me and wrapped his arms around me in a hug. "You cannot blame yourself for his death," he whispered. "He would not want you to. He died doing something he loved, protecting you, and he should be remembered for his heroism."

"If I hadn't…" I started.

"Enough," Hera said. "You will not blame yourself." She walked to me and grabbed my chin in her hands. "Grieve for your lost one and then square your shoulders and rule as the Queen that you are. You have priorities and you must not act so disparagingly about the war."

"There's something I have to tell you," I said.

She released me and frowned. "What has happened?"

"Maurice is immune to sunlight."

Zeus and Hera's eyes widened and she asked, "How do you know this?"

"I attacked him," I said. "I used sunlight on him, and he sat in it, examining his fingernails."

"Hope is not lost for the war," Zeus said, "He is still vulnerable to fire."

"I fear I cannot defeat him," I whispered. "He is too strong."

"We will figure something out," Zeus assured me. "I have already called a meeting and hopefully there we will formulate a plan."

Ares returned empty handed. "Are you ready to leave?" he asked me.

"Leave, where?" I asked.

"To eat. Come, you need to eat and then rest," Ares said softly.

I let him lead me away from Zeus and Hera, wanting to get away from Achilles' body before I started crying again. I knew I should ask Ares if he was mad at me about Achilles, but I was too chicken to ask, fearing his answer. I was surprised and relieved that Hera and Zeus did not blame me and would take Hera's instructions to heart. She was right, I had to lead as the Queen of the Werewolves. There were many more lives at stake than my own.

SEVEN

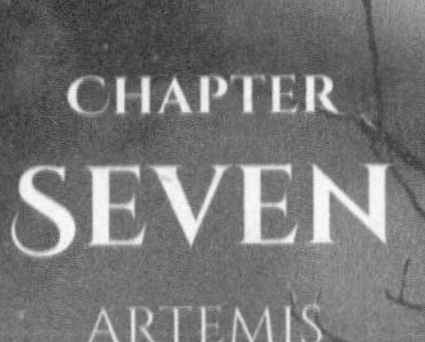

"Why are you sad?" Achilles asked me softly as he stroked my hair. We were in a beautiful meadow with a softly bubbling brook a few yards away. The sun was warm against my face and a soft wind caressed my skin. How could it feel so right when everything was wrong?

"You're dead," I whispered miserably as I lay in the comfort of his arms. "I will never see you again."

He smiled and whispered, "I will always be with you, Artemis. I live inside of you and Ares. I am a part of your past which has shaped your future. As long as you do not forget, I will always be with you."

"I will never forget you. I love you," I whispered as I looked up at him.

He pressed his lips against my forehead and whispered, "Then live, Artemis. Fulfill the prophecy, raise children with Ares, and live your life. I will always be in your heart and your memories. That is the best any man could ask for. Do not blame your brother for my death but embrace him and reconcile, as Ares and I did after so many years. Do not make the same mistakes as we did. Remember, *verus amor vincit omnia.* True love conquers all. Fulfill the prophecy and right the balance of light and darkness."

"Achilles!" I yelled as the dream dissolved and I opened my eyes to find Koda and Ares looking at me. I wrapped my arms around Ares and cried, needing to be comforted by him despite feeling like it might be wrong.

Koda wrapped his body around me from behind and my two-man pack comforted me.

After several minutes, I calmed myself and wiped the remaining tears from my eyes. "I'm sorry," I whispered.

Koda rubbed my back slowly and Ares kissed my cheek.

"You have nothing to apologize for," Ares answered. My stomach growled and Ares said, "That's our cue to get you food. Come, on, let's eat."

I really wanted to just lie in bed and weep for the loss of Achilles. I wanted to let my body release the pain it was feeling in some way, but Achilles did not want me to lie around. He wanted me to live, so that was exactly what I was going to do. I would not hide in my room and weep. I would use the time I had to plan and seek revenge on Maurice for Achilles' life.

I looked around in shock as I realized that we weren't in the cathedral anymore, but in a room with a bed. "Where are we?"

"We are in Zeus' realm," Ares answered.

"How did we get here? When?" I asked, feeling like I had missed something.

"After you ate last night you fell asleep and Victor teleported us here," Koda said.

"I don't remember eating," I admitted.

Ares and Koda looked at each other but did not say anything.

A servant brought in plates piled high with food. I ate until I couldn't hold any more and then changed into clothes I found in the dresser.

"You should visit the dragons today. They have been waiting patiently, but I am not sure how much longer their patience will last," Ares said softly.

"Blu's here?" I gasped, turning away from the mirror where I had been staring at my haggard self. I was in desperate need of a shower.

"He is not far, but not in this realm. He felt you die and flew to the cathedral. According to Victor, Blu is the reason I survived," Ares said.

Without another word I flung open the bedroom door and ran down the hallway towards the exit.

Ares raced after me and caught up to me just as I pushed open the outside doors.

"Wait for me," Koda called from behind us.

I grabbed each of their hands and then asked, "Where to?"

"We are simply walking out of the passage," Ares said.

I dropped their hands, raced up the stairs, and flung open the hatch.

Blu roared from the sky where he had been circling and dove to the ground, landing heavily and making me wobble. Ares steadied me with a hand on my shoulder and then released me.

Blu wrapped his neck around me, humming loudly. "Hatchling, I have been worried about you," he said in his deep and familiar voice.

I wrapped my arms around as much of his neck as I could. "Thank you for coming, Blu. I have missed you greatly."

He backed away from me and said, "I am sorry for the loss of your bound Sidhe. He would have been a great king."

I sniffed as tears threatened to leak out. "Thank you."

Ares picked my hand up, helping drive away the sadness by his comfort.

Zeus stepped out of the portal and smiled when he saw me. He walked to me and wrapped me in the biggest hug I had ever received, other than Blu's. "Artemis, I am so glad to see you."

"Sorry about the other day and going a little crazy with my powers," I whispered, warmth heating my cheeks.

He shook his head and pulled back, holding me by the arms. "Do not apologize for grieving over my son. I expected nothing less." Zeus looked at Ares and said, "The ceremony will begin in one hour. Will you assist me?"

Ares bowed at the waist. "It would be an honor."

"What are you talking about?" I asked softly.

"The funeral," Zeus answered.

I leaned my head against Zeus' chest. "When do we get to kill vampires again?"

Zeus squeezed my shoulders. "Killing your enemies is always more fun than burning your loved ones. We will resume the fun soon."

Blu asked, "Would the Sidhe mind if some non-Sidhe attended the ceremony?"

Zeus turned and smiled at Draco Blu. "The Sidhe would be honored if the dragons attended. I'm guessing you are more interested in the announcement at the end?"

Blu nodded once. "Yes, we know your protocol and are interested in the announcement after the funeral. Plus, we would like to pay our respects to Achilles."

Ares tugged on my hand. "Come on, we need to get changed."

Zeus kissed my cheek and released me. "I will see you both in an hour."

Ares led me back to the room where Victor was waiting for us. Victor stood when he saw me enter and enveloped me in a hug. "*Mon papillon.* It is good to see you breathing and not getting yourself into trouble."

I hugged the vampire back and then stepped out of his arms. "How long did you see me not breathing?"

"He stayed at yours and Ares' sides the entire time," Koda answered from the chair he had sat down in.

I looked at Victor. "You did?"

Victor shrugged. "It is not important."

He was hiding something, but I let it go since Koda needed comforting. I sat on his lap and let him cradle me for a moment, not long enough to be rude to Ares, but also not too short to worry Koda. Ares held out a black dress and advised the others of the funeral time.

After putting on the dress and tying my hair up, I sat on the edge of the bed pondering over everything. In order to fulfill the prophecy, I had to restore the balance of good and evil, of light and darkness. To do that I had to defeat Maurice. To do that I had to destroy most of his vampires. I knew what I had to do, but to effectively do it I needed my brother's help. "Ares?"

Ares turned around, finishing buttoning up his black dress shirt. "Yes?"

"Where's Apollo?"

Koda snarled and Ares asked, "Why do you want to know?"

I exhaled and said, "I had a dream and Achilles told me not to blame my brother and to embrace him."

Ares stopped his buttoning and said, "He's locked in a dungeon cell right now. Even if he had never meant to harm you, he killed Achilles. The Sidhe aren't going to just let that go."

"Are they going to execute him?" I asked nervously.

Ares looked at Victor who said, "They haven't told me anything, but I think they were waiting for your return before making the final decision. I'm sure they will make the decision tomorrow though."

I exhaled. "Okay."

Ares looked at Victor again and Victor shook his head. "I have no clue who they're going to choose."

"Choose for what?" I asked feeling left out yet again. It was a problem that happened far too often with this group and was something I intended to fix.

Ares smiled. "You'll just have to find out with the rest of us after the funeral."

I rolled my eyes and followed him out of the room. He led our small group out the back of the building and to a large wooden platform. Wood was piled high underneath it and an enormous crowd, consisting mostly of Sidhe, had gathered.

Victor and Koda joined the crowd and Ares pulled me off to the side. "I'm going to be part of the procession, so you should go stand beside Hera."

I kissed his cheek before making my way through the crowd to Hera.

Athena stood beside Hera and when she saw me, she lunged forward and wrapped her arms around me. "Artemis, I am so sorry for how I have treated you. Please, forgive me."

I patted my mother awkwardly on the back and then

released the anger that had begun simmering at her presence and hugged her back. "You're forgiven."

Athena smiled at me and kissed my cheek. "Thank you."

I took my place next to Hera who acknowledged my presence by grabbing my hand in hers, her grip tightened until it was almost painful, but I said nothing. Athena stood on Hera's other side and Hera latched on to her just as quickly.

A horn trumpeted and all of the Sidhe released their wings from their backs. Athena nodded at me, and I released mine as well, letting my body glow with the rest of the Sidhe.

Zeus began singing and then Ares joined him. I had never heard Zeus sing and was surprised at how wonderful they sounded. They sang a sorrowful song in a language I could not understand and carried Achilles' body on a plank towards the wooden platform in front of where we were all standing. The sight of father and son singing brought back a memory of Ares and Achilles singing to me in Hera's court what was probably only a few weeks ago but felt like years.

The Sidhe in the crowd joined the song one by one until all of the full blooded Sidhe were singing their sorrow and mourning together. Even Hera sang, her voice carrying above the others in her extreme grief. I had never before heard something so eerily beautiful and at the same time heart-breaking. I didn't need to know the words to know that they were singing their mourning for Achilles.

The song stopped as Zeus and Ares laid Achilles' body on top of the platform. Zeus turned to Ares and Ares' body began to glow, and he created fire in his hand. He dropped the fire onto the wood and then walked to me, his body still glowing as mine was. He took my free hand as tears streamed down his face.

I cried in silence with the rest of the Sidhe as we watched until the fire died.

The crowd turned as Zeus flew up into the air near the building. "As is customary after the death and funeral of the heir, I will announce my new heir. Hera, please join me." Hera released Athena and my hands and flew up into the air beside her husband, taking his hand. Zeus smiled at her, but she simply nodded at him. "Achilles was the heir to both the dark and light courts. Therefore, a new heir for both of the courts needs to be chosen. In the past, each court has been allowed to choose a separate heir, but Hera and I have decided to choose a joint heir again."

The crowd was thrumming with anticipation at the announcement. I only felt exhausted and sad.

"I, Zeus, King of the Dark Court of the Sidhe, with the consent of Hera, Queen of the Light Court of the Sidhe, hereby declare that Artemis Lupine is the new heir to both the Light and Dark Courts of the Sidhe."

Of all of the surprised gasps, mine must have been the loudest. Ares squeezed my hand and whispered. "If you accept, you need to fly up to them."

I stared at him, unable to process this. "I...I..." How could they spring this on me? Why hadn't they talked to me about it before? Wasn't Ares technically the next heir?

He released my hand and smiled. "It's what Achilles would have wanted."

I exhaled and flapped my wings, pushing myself up into the air and flying to Zeus and Hera. I hovered in front of them and said the only thing that I could in the situation, "I accept this great honor."

Hera was handed a purple bag and from it she pulled a small tiara. "We are glad that you accept and will do our best to prepare you well before your ascension to the throne." She placed the tiara on my head and whispered a spell which released a block that had been on the tiara. Power flowed from the tiara into me and then memories of past bearers of the tiara began to stream into my head. I closed the barrier as I had learned to do before, and the memories stopped. My right ring finger began to tingle and then a small tattoo appeared around it.

I turned to face the crowd and Zeus said, "All hail Princess Artemis, Heir to the Sidhe Throne!"

The crowd dropped to their knees and bowed with their foreheads touching the ground, everyone except Victor, Ares and Draco Blu. Victor, Ares and Blu did bow their heads in respect though.

I swallowed nervously and prayed that I could live up to their expectations. As long as Ares was by my side, I knew we could get through this together.

EIGHT

"No, I won't allow him to be executed!" I yelled at Zeus.

Zeus was trying to control his anger, but bits of his power flared. "He killed Achilles, the Prince of the Sidhe. There is no punishment, except death, harsh enough for such an act. If we let him off easy, then others will attempt the same thing."

I turned to Ares, who sat beside me. "There has to be something. Please. Help me."

Ares rubbed the stubble on his chin and said, "I might have an idea, but it's not something we have used in generations. It was considered too barbaric by the Sidhe. It may be fitting for the current situation though."

Zeus looked at Ares a moment and exhaled. "Have you even talked to him? Do we even know if he wants to switch sides? He *was* a servant of Maurice's."

"He didn't know!" I said through clenched teeth. "Darren gave him to Maurice's people to raise. He saved me and killed Darren and surrendered after I died. That has to count for something."

Ares rested his hand on my arm and tried to calm me with our bond, but I pushed his hand off and paced across the room.

"I will speak to him and determine if he is willing to pledge loyalty to Artemis. If he is, and he makes the vow, then will you agree to the punishment I speak of?" Ares asked.

"I don't even know the punishment," I said in irritation.

Ares whispered, "I was asking Zeus."

I blushed and looked down at my hands. "Oh."

Zeus frowned a moment and then exhaled. "The others will not like it, but I do believe it is a severe enough punishment. Speak with him and return. Artemis and I need to discuss other matters anyways."

Ares stood, kissed my cheek and left. I sat down in the chair next to Zeus and exhaled. "I don't like making decisions."

Zeus laughed. "It gets easier with age and practice."

"That is hard to believe," I muttered.

"Artemis, as heir you do not have to make decisions, but I think it would be good for you to at least weigh in on the topics and listen to Hera and I making decisions. You know that you won't need to take over our reign until we die, which won't be for a long time unless there are extenuating circumstances."

"Can we not talk about your deaths? There has been enough already."

He rested his hand on my shoulder and smiled. "Soon we will finish this war and you will raise your child in happy times."

I rested my hand on my stomach and asked, "What if I can't do it? What if I can't defeat Maurice?"

"There is not a doubt in my mind that you will. He has

grown arrogant these past one hundred years. You will be able to defeat him. You just have to figure out how."

He made it sound like it was a simple task. How do you kill a vampire who is the one of the most powerful in the world? Fire, but that would mean getting close enough and cornering him to use it. Plus, I was sure that he had ways to protect himself from fire if he had survived this long.

"Artemis," Zeus said softly, "Why don't you go rest? We can discuss everything else later."

I was tired, but there was too much at stake. Too much that still needed to be done, like killing Maurice. I had thought many times about popping back into his chambers and toasting him and popping back out, without anyone knowing. But I couldn't risk my life like I had been willing to before. It was strange to know a being was growing and living inside me, but I had accepted it and vowed to be the best mother that I could be.

"Alright, I'll rest, but we still need to figure out our plan for attacking Maurice. The world has lived in darkness too long, and I don't want to raise my child in it," I said to Zeus as I stood. I stopped at the door and said, "I do have one more question though."

"What is it?" Zeus asked.

"Why did you make me heir when Ares was already the next in line? Why isn't he now the heir?" Zeus had held a feast in his honor, naming Ares an heir to the throne so it did not make sense to me.

"Normally Ares would have become the next heir for the Dark Throne, but that still left the Light Throne open. Ares, Hera and I discussed it and we all agreed that you were the best person to be our heir, besides, Ares is your mate so naturally he would be your king which would still allow him to be heir."

I frowned. "So, Hera did not want Ares to be heir to her throne is what you are saying."

Zeus exhaled. "My wife holds grudges and unfortunately Ares has received much of her wrath because of my indiscretion with his mother. She is making strides to stop being so one sided when it comes to Ares, but it will take her time. This is a great step for her."

Great was not really the word I was thinking, but I let it pass.

Koda followed me out of the room and towards Ares' old chambers, which Zeus had given us. "How are you feelin', Darlin'?"

He was always asking me that. Ever since I had returned from being dead, he had renewed his job as my guard and stuck to me like glue. "I'm fine, Koda. I am just tired and queasy."

"Do you want me to get a healer?" he asked.

I shook my head. "It's just morning sickness. Maybe I need to try to eat something?"

"I'll get her some food," Victor said from beside me.

I refrained from jumping or yelling in surprise, but knew I couldn't lie to him mentally since he could read minds. "Not funny," I grumbled.

Victor smiled. "I didn't mean to startle you. What would you like to eat?"

He had also been incredibly nice to me since I had returned, not that he wasn't always nice, but everyone treated me differently now that I was pregnant. Like I was a porcelain doll that needed to be pampered or I would start crying.

"Fruits and cheeses would be nice," I said with a smile. "Thank you."

He kissed my cheek and then disappeared in a flash, using his ability to teleport. If only I could use that ability to my advantage against Maurice.

Koda pushed open the door to the bedroom and I waited patiently as he searched inside to ensure that it was safe for me to enter. It frustrated me that he insisted on doing this since I was more powerful than him and extremely capable of protecting myself. I hadn't died because I was careless.

My throat constricted at the memory of Achilles' death and tears filled in my eyes.

Koda stepped out to tell me it was safe and saw my face. "Darlin', let's lie down while we wait for Victor to return."

I nodded and wiped at my eyes, but that seemed to only open the flood gates.

Koda took my hand, led me to the bed, and curled up around me as soon as I lay down. "I know it hurts. I'm sorry."

"I miss him so much," I whispered. And I felt awful for how our relationship had been. I had tortured him emotionally and physically with our bond that we never sealed.

"He wouldn't want you to blame yourself," Victor said as he set a tray of food down at the end of the bed and touched my arm. "He knows why you made the choices that you did, and he never blamed you."

If anyone else would have said it, I wouldn't have believed them, but Victor was one of the few who actually knew what people were thinking and feeling.

"Will it ever stop hurting?" I asked.

"No," Victor said seriously.

"Victor," Koda hissed his name.

Victor smiled. "No, it will never stop, but it will turn into a low ache that you can deal with. You must focus on the positive memories. Remember how much he loved you and how much you loved him. Remember the fun times you had together and soon it will be bearable."

"He's right," Koda said. "As much as I loved Matt, now his death is simply a dull ache within my chest. If you focus on the good times, you can get through it."

"Come and eat. The baby is sure to be hungry," Victor said as he softly tugged on my hand.

I sat up and did as he asked. "Thank you."

Victor sat in one of the chairs in the room and closed his eyes. "You are welcome."

"Victor?" I asked softly.

"Hm?"

"The prophecy says that I am the one to restore the balance of good and evil, but it doesn't specifically say who is supposed to kill Maurice. He's your father and... Are you planning on killing him or should I be?"

Victor kept his eyes closed, but his lips lifted up into a wide smile, showing the lower part of his fangs. "As the next in line for the throne it doesn't matter if I kill him or not, but I would prefer if I killed him. However, he has caused you an enormous amount of misery, so I would understand if you wanted to kill him."

"That didn't answer my question," I said, eating some of the food he had brought me.

He shrugged and folded his hands in his lap. "We shall see when the battle starts, *mon papillon*. Then we shall decide."

I couldn't argue with that, so I lay down instead of trying to find an answer now.

Koda wrapped himself around me again. "Sleep, Artemis. Sleep and I will protect you."

"Two weeks," I whispered. "I want to fight Maurice and his group in two weeks."

"We will discuss it later," Koda said sternly. "Rest or I'll call Hades in here."

"Alright," I said as I snuggled against him. "Koda, promise me something?"

"Anything," he whispered.

"Don't let Ares die."

"Darlin' I've been trying to keep him alive since I was ten," he said and chuckled.

"I'm not strong enough to raise this child without him. I can't lose anyone else. I can't lose Ares or you," I said and sniffled.

"Go to sleep, Artemis," he whispered. "Everyone will be safe while you sleep."

I closed my eyes and sighed. "Okay, but only for an hour or two."

"Artemis," Ares whispered as he ran his hand along my stomach. "Wake up, Sunshine."

"So tired," I whispered as I opened my eyes.

Ares smiled down at me. "I know, but you need to eat. It sounds like the baby is roaring in your stomach."

I sat up and then fell back. My body was burning up, like I was covered in blankets. "It's so hot," I whispered.

Ares ran his hand over my forehead and then yelled, "Healer!"

The healer from the feast hurried into the room. She put her hand on my head and stomach and frowned. "She has a strange illness. We must get rid of this fever before it begins to affect the baby."

"Ares," I whispered as the healer began chanting. "Don't leave me."

He gripped one of my hands with his and stroked my hair. "Never."

After a few moments, the fever began to dissipate and the strange lightheadedness I had been feeling disappeared.

"How do you feel?" the healer asked me.

"Much better, thank you," I said as Ares helped me sit up and handed me a cup of water to drink.

"Ares, a word please," the healer said as she headed towards the door.

Ares kissed my hand and followed the healer outside the chambers.

Even though I had slept for at least three hours, I felt exhausted again. What was wrong with me? Preternaturals never got sick. Was there something wrong with the baby?

Ares stepped back into the room and smiled at me. "Don't worry. She said the baby is perfectly healthy and you are now as well."

He was telling the truth.

I exhaled. "Okay."

"But she did order you to stay in bed today."

"All day?" I asked, my mouth dropped open.

He nodded. "Yes. She doesn't want you overexerting yourself and possibly hurting the baby."

"What good is it to be a preternatural if I can't even get out of bed?" I grumbled with a frown.

He sat down next to me and began massaging my shoulders. "With your metabolism, whatever got into your system will be gone soon. Plus, it gives us an excuse to cuddle all day," he said as he continued his massage.

"Maybe it's not so bad after all," I murmured as I relaxed more and more from his expert hands.

Ares kissed the back of my shoulder and moved his hands down to my back. "Are you hungry?" he asked.

"Yes, but I don't want you to leave," I admitted to him.

"I won't. I'll just summon Koda."

"Where is he?" I asked, shocked he hadn't stayed glued to my side.

Ares' fingers kneaded the knots around my shoulder blades. "I sent him away when I came in. I wanted some alone time with you."

"Alone time? What's that?" I asked as I leaned back against him, smirking.

He wrapped his arms around my upper chest and sighed. "Yes, it is a very scarce commodity for us. Soon, we will end this war and then we will have all the alone time we want."

"You're dreaming," I told him. "With you as Alpha of the Werewolves, and me as Heir to the Sidhe thrones, we will *never* have alone time."

Ares laughed. "I suppose you're right. That just means that we have to treasure every alone moment we have."

"You summoned?" Koda asked as he walked in.

"Can you get me some food? I'm on bed rest so I can't get up," I answered.

"Bed rest?" he asked with worry evident in his voice.

"Easy, she just had a fever and the healer wanted to be sure she and the baby were fine, so she ordered bed rest," Ares said reassuringly as he ran his hands down my arms.

"What do you want to eat?" Koda asked.

I thought about some of my options and then nausea

spiked, and I had to jump up and run to the bathroom to throw up.

"Crackers and water would be good," Ares told Koda as he came to me and pulled my hair back.

My stomach finally stopped convulsing, but I was still exhausted, so I just leaned against the toilet. "I'm so glad Zeus has indoor plumbing," I whispered.

Ares laughed softly and stroked my back. "Who do you think invented it?"

"How's Apollo?" I asked him as I leaned back against his chest.

"He's fine."

"Did he agree to whatever it was you and Zeus were talking about?" I asked.

Ares rested his chin on top of my head. "I gave him until tomorrow to decide."

"And what exactly is he deciding to?"

"It's difficult to explain, but basically he would be pledging himself to my service for the rest of his life."

"You're making him a slave?" I asked, horrified, and pulled away from him.

Ares sighed. "He would only be a slave by the spell, but I wouldn't actually force him to be a slave for us."

"That's awful," I whispered and pulled away from Ares to stand up, gripping the sink to keep from falling from my dizziness.

"It's the only way Zeus will allow him to continue to live. It's either that or he's killed for his crimes," Ares said matter-of-factly.

I brushed my teeth and then walked back to bed, lying on my side.

Why were things always so easy for Ares? Kill or be killed.

Punish him by death or slavery. I couldn't think that way all the time. Especially not about people I loved.

"I want to attack Maurice in two weeks," I told him.

"So soon?" he asked as he settled behind me. "I had hoped you would allow more time for you to recuperate."

"I want this war over before the baby is born. I want the world to have some semblance of balance before we bring a newborn into it," I told him.

Ares rested his hand on my stomach and sighed happily. "I hope it's a boy."

I laughed. "All men want boys."

"That's because we want to raise a man to take our place."

"Well I don't care what gender it is. I just want it to be healthy and safe," I said and looked down at my stomach.

"I'll rip off anyone's arm who even tries to touch it," Ares said with a menacing growl.

"I'm sure no one would be that stupid."

Ares kissed my neck. "Many have tried to hurt you," he whispered.

I closed my eyes as I relaxed against him. "Yes, and we've killed them all."

"Not all, we still have Maurice."

"Yes, Maurice, but soon enough…I will kill him."

"I don't want you fighting. I can't lose you and our baby again," he whispered as he rubbed my stomach and kissed my neck. "I'll go crazy and Zeus will have to put me down," he said softly.

I set my hand on top of his on my stomach. "I must fight. I must right the balance. I must end Maurice's life."

"Can't we wait at least until after you have the baby?" he suggested. "Then if you are determined to fight, we could ensure our child was safe somewhere."

"Food's here," Koda said as he entered the room again with a tray of cheese and crackers. "I figured you would be ready to eat by now."

I sat up and took a piece of cheese, chewing on the soft and delicious goodness. "Thank you."

Koda sat down on the end of the bed and looked at Ares. "Mother is here," he said softly. "She asked to see you privately."

Ares sighed. "I was hoping not to have to deal with this until later. Did she seem mad?"

Koda shrugged. "Not particularly."

"I'm not leaving Artemis' side, so bring her here to our chambers. I'm sure we can manage to be civil," Ares said.

Koda nodded and then looked at me. "You alright now? You need anything else?"

"There aren't any *Sprites* lying around are there?" I asked hopefully, but already knew the answer.

"Sprites? You mean little pixie beings?"

I laughed. "No, lemon-lime soda. You know, from the human era."

Koda laughed. "Oh that. I'll see what I can dig up."

"You're the best," I said as I chewed on my cheese.

Koda winked. "I know."

Ares laughed at his brother's conceitedness and then stole a piece of my cheese. "Stolen food always tastes so much better," Ares said with a wicked smirk.

I growled. "My food."

Ares growled back, but there was no real anger in his growl. "Everything that is yours is mine."

"Haven't you ever heard the line, 'what's his is hers and what's hers is hers'?"

Ares lifted his lips in a playful snarl. "Not when I'm involved."

"So territorial," I said as I snatched the last little bit of cheese he had stolen and popped it into my mouth.

He wrapped his arms around me. "You're mine."

I laughed. "Yes, I'm yours. All yours," I said softly as my sadness over Achilles' death returned.

"I miss him, too," Ares whispered.

Someone knocked on the door, breaking the mood thankfully. I

stood up and walked to the restroom, closing and locking the door.

"Enter," Ares said.

"So commanding," his mother, Beatrice, said as she entered. I stared at my reflection, unsure if I was ready to face her again.

"It's great to finally see you, Mother," Ares said to her.

I opened the door but stayed just out of sight to see how their meeting went.

He walked to her and hugged her.

She hugged him, but as soon as they separated, she slapped his cheek. "That is for killing my mate."

I growled softly, not liking seeing her slap him, but stayed still.

"He challenged me," Ares said. "I had no choice but to kill him. I am sorry for any grief I have caused you."

"You should have killed him one hundred and fifty years ago," she said angrily. "How could you leave me in his hands for so long?"

Ares gaped at her. "You never told me you were unhappy. You never acted unhappy."

"I couldn't act unhappy in front of him," she said. "I was a queen. I had to keep our people united."

"You could have told me," Ares snapped. "If I had known, I would have killed him. I thought you loved him."

"How could I love him? He killed my mate!" she screamed.

"Mother," Koda chastised. "You should have told us."

She inhaled, and her queenly face was back on. "I'm sorry. I let my emotions get the better of me."

Ares smiled at her. "It's understandable."

I stepped out of the bathroom and walked to Ares' side. "Hello."

Beatrice looked at me and then blinked twice. "Wait? Isn't she supposed to be dead?"

"She was dead," Koda said. "But Ares retrieved her soul from Death."

"My soul and our child's," I said as I rested a hand on my stomach.

Her eyes widened and she looked from my stomach to Ares. "A child?"

"Yes, you're going to be a grandmother," Ares told her as he put his arm around my hips.

"You are sure that it is yours?" she asked Ares with narrowed eyes at my stomach.

I growled. "How dare you insinuate I have cheated on Ares. I would never cheat on my mate. Even if I am a half-breed, half of me is still a wolf."

She smiled at me. "I like her. She's feisty."

"Yes, very," Ares said as though exasperated.

I pinched his arm. "Don't be rude."

"May I?" she asked as she pointed at my stomach.

I looked at Ares, unsure what she wanted. "She wants to speak to the baby."

"Oh. Sure," I said and pulled my hands out of the way.

She crouched down and put her ear against my stomach. The smell of lilacs and wolf fur drifted up to me and I realized that it was Beatrice's scent. "My, what a loud heartbeat you have, little one. You must grow strong and big. You are going to be the Alpha someday." She was quiet a moment and then whispered, "You will be protected from harm. None shall hurt you. Do not worry. None shall hurt you or your mother ever again." She stood up and met Ares' eyes. "I'm joining you in the battle against Maurice."

"No," he said definitively.

Beatrice snarled at him, and her eyes turned amber. "Even if you are old and powerful, I birthed you. I created your power within me. You cannot stop me."

Ares' eyes had turned amber as well, but after a moment of staring at his mother, they finally returned to normal. "You're as stubborn as ever."

She patted his cheek softly. "Good boy. Alright, I'm off to find a room."

"I'll escort you," Koda said with a wide smile and held the door open for his mother.

"Such a good boy," she said as she kissed his cheek and placed her hand on his bent elbow. "Goodbye, Artemis. Keep Ares in check while I am gone."

The door closed and I turned to Ares with a wide smile. "I like her."

Ares laughed. "Of course, you do, now get back in bed."

"Yes, master," I said in a mocking tone as I sat on the edge to continue eating.

We remained sitting in silence for a few minutes, and then Ares said, "Artemis, I have wanted to ask you something since you came back but have not found the right opportunity."

"You know you can ask me anything," I told him and turned to face him.

"Do you remember being dead?" he asked. "Do you remember anything after you died, I mean?"

I shook my head. "No. I remember seeing Achilles fall and then my strength gave out and I dropped to the ground. Then I woke up when I came back to life."

"Good," Ares said with evident relief as his shoulders relaxed.

"Were you worried I had been frightened while in Death's realm?" I asked and placed a hand on his shoulder.

He picked my hand up and placed it against his cheek. "Yes."

I smiled. "I wasn't. Even when I died, I wasn't scared. It all happened too fast."

"I'm sorry."

I rubbed his cheek with my thumb. "Don't apologize. You saved me from Death. That is the bravest thing I have ever heard."

He stared into my eyes and said, "I love you."

I smiled wide. "I love you too, Ares and I always will. Even when you're being a stubborn, pain in my butt or trying to order me around. I will always love you."

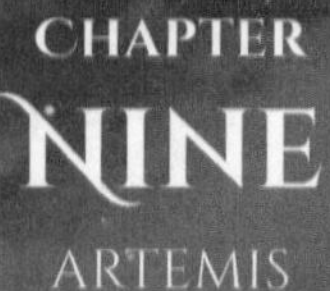

One week of nothing was driving me insane. The healer came to check on me every day and though my fever had stayed away I was still exhausted and dizzy quite often. She wasn't sure what to make of it and gathered a council of healers to discuss the matter.

Being trapped in my room was not fun and brought back so many memories of prior times in my life with Ares.

Finally, the healer said that as long as Ares kept his arm around me in case I fainted, I could go for a walk.

So, we strolled through the Dark Court along the beach and watched as dolphins played in the sea with water nymphs.

"When this is all over, where will we live?" I asked Ares as we walked, and I shuffled my feet in the warm sand.

He tilted his head back and let the sun highlight his handsome face a moment. "Well, that's something I have not thought about yet. I own multiple properties in several countries."

"I guess we will just have to travel to each one until I find the one I like," I said with a smile.

Ares looked down at me with a wide smile. "Sounds like a plan to me."

"Will my pregnancy be nine months?" I asked him, having forgotten to ask sooner.

"No, it will be three months."

"And I am already one month?" My eyes widened at the realization that delivery was going to be much sooner than I had anticipated.

"Actually, you are starting on your second month in three days."

I didn't really believe him since my stomach was still flat, but I did not say that.

"What if I can't defeat Maurice? What if I can't right the balance?"

"Then you will teleport us to Darren's old house, and from there we will travel around until we find a place to live, alone and safely," he said like it was an easy plan.

"Hm," I mumbled, not wanting to say anything because I would not teleport and leave everyone to die. I couldn't do that.

"We should head back. It's time for the meeting with Zeus," Ares said and pivoted us back towards the castle.

Birds high up in the sky circled lazily.

I was watching their circles when something extremely larger than them dove and scattered them. "Ares!" I gasped and pointed. "What is that?"

Ares looked up and watched the flying animal a moment before laughing. "That is an old friend. Would you like to meet him?"

"A friend?" I asked.

Ares put two fingers in his mouth and whistled.

The flying being swerved away from the birds it had been

chasing and headed in our direction. The body moved away from the sun, and I could finally see the shape.

"A Pegasus?" I asked. I had assumed that there were other preternatural beings alive that I had not met yet, but I had never dreamed I would meet a Pegasus.

The Pegasus in question landed and bobbed its head at Ares. "Ares! It's been so long!"

I kept my mouth closed even though my jaw wanted to hit the ground. How could a Pegasus, with a horse head, speak English?

Ares scratched its ears affectionately. "I've missed you as well, Starling."

"Who is this?" Starling asked as he bobbed his head towards me and nickered. "She's pretty."

"Starling, I would like you to meet Artemis Lupine, my mate."

Starling snorted and opened his eyes wide. "This is the infamous Artemis Lupine? It's an honor to meet you." Starling lowered the front half of his body in a bow.

"Thank you, it's an honor to meet you, Starling," I managed to say like I wasn't still reeling in shock.

Starling stood up and then tilted his head sideways to look at Ares. "Need a ride?"

Ares smiled. "Actually, we would love a ride. Artemis is pregnant and a bit wobbly on her feet at the moment."

"Hop on!" Starling encouraged. "I'll take you to the castle."

Ares helped me on and then hopped onto Starling's back behind me, holding me against his chest. "Hold on to the mane," Ares whispered.

"Here we go," Starling said and then started running down the beach. Sand kicked up around us, wind pressed against my face and the water sprayed us softly.

After running a little ways Starling leapt and flapped his wings, carrying us into the air. "You seem a little out of shape, old friend," Ares teased.

"You seem to have gained some weight," Starling said back.

I laughed and Ares said, "I've only gained muscle."

"Or perhaps it's the fat in your head," Starling said and then whinnied loudly in Pegasus laughter.

"Ha. Ha," Ares said. "You are as funny now as you were four hundred years ago."

"How long does a Pegasus live?" I asked, my eyes widening.

"As long as we want," Starling answered. "Some of us prefer to live a normal horse's age while others, like me, enjoy living a long life."

Starling landed in front of the castle and Ares hopped off and then lifted me from Starling's back and set me down on the ground.

"Thank you," Ares said and bowed.

Starling nudged Ares' chest. "Anytime. You take care of your baby."

"I will."

We watched Starling fly away again before walking into the castle.

"That was fun," I said. "I've always wanted to meet a Pegasus."

"If you didn't have wings of your own, I would suggest getting one, but then you would not be able to use your own wings."

"Yeah, I would much rather use my own," I admitted.

We walked down the large hallways and into the gathering room where the meeting for the battle was being held. Hera, Zeus, Beatrice, and Koda were standing off to the side talking while the rest of the people sat in seats murmuring.

"Chandra," said a voice I had missed deeply.

I turned to my right and a smile split my face. "Selene!" I said with a smile, pulled away from Ares and hugged her. "I've missed you."

"I have missed you as well, sister. How fare you? I had heard that you were dead and couldn't believe the rumors," she said as she smiled at me. She wore a beautiful black and purple dress with moons embroidered on it.

"Well, I did die, but then came back and we found out that I'm pregnant." I grinned.

Selene's shock was quick and then she smiled again. "How wonderful that you are with child. We must catch up after the meeting."

"Of course," I said and stepped back into Ares' arm.

"Artemis," Zeus called. "Please come up here."

Ares and I walked to the front of the room where they were standing, and Koda pulled out a chair for me next to Beatrice.

Ares sat beside me, and Koda took his position behind my chair as my guard.

The room quieted and people took seats in the audience.

"As you all know, the upcoming battle with Maurice and his followers will not be an easy one. This battle will determine the fate of the world," Zeus began.

Victor popped into the room in the back with Dmitri beside him and Victor winked at me in hello.

Damn flirtatious vampire. I thought at him.

He smiled wide, flashing his fangs and walked forward.

"Victor, thank you for joining us," Zeus said as Victor took a seat beside Ares up front.

"My pleasure," Victor said. Dmitri stood behind Victor like

a bodyguard but smiled pleasantly at me when he saw me looking at him.

"We're calling in all the help we can get," Zeus continued. "We are continuing to add to our allies and we're planning a battle like none before. I would like to welcome Selene and her fellow witches."

Selene bowed her head respectfully. "Thank you for contacting us. We look forward to the battle ahead."

"We welcome the Elves and Alianna, their leader."

A silver haired, pointed eared Elf stood up and bowed. "Thank you."

I hadn't even noticed the group until then, but now I could see at least two dozen elves in the audience.

I needed to pay better attention to my surroundings.

"We welcome the Dwarves and their leader, Klaus."

"Thank you," the leader, one of the midgets with thick beards, said in very rough English.

"We welcome the Trolls and their leader, Razi."

The troll leader stood up and up and up. He was well over ten feet tall. "Thank you," he said in an elegant British accent despite the tusks in his mouth.

How had I not seen any of these creatures in here before now? I was seriously lacking on my observation skills.

"And we welcome the Shapeshifters and Wereanimals of every group and their leaders."

Ten women and men stood up and bowed.

I had so many questions for Ares, but I could not ask any of them. I needed a notepad to write them all down.

"Let me introduce those here in the front. I am Zeus, King of the Dark Court of the Sidhe. This is Hera, Queen of the Light Court of the Sidhe. To her left is Beatrice, former Alpha female of the Werewolves. To her left is Artemis, Alpha female of the Werewolves and Heir to the Sidhe throne." Several of those gathered murmured loudly, but Zeus continued. "To her left is Ares, Alpha of the Werewolves and Artemis' mate. To his left is Victor, Prince of the Vampires."

Razi, leader of the Trolls, stood up. "I do not mean to sound stupid, but I had heard Artemis had died." His voice was rough and deep, and it hurt my ears a little.

"She did die," Ares answered.

"Yet she is sitting beside you?" the Troll asked, obviously perplexed.

"Ares reclaimed my soul from Death," I explained.

"Death gave your soul up?" Alianna asked, eyes wide.

"Yes, mine and my child's," I answered.

The audience began murmuring even louder.

"How do we know this isn't just a trick? That Artemis isn't still dead and that you are not just going to lead us straight to our deaths? How do we know you aren't lying, Zeus?" asked another of the Elves angrily.

Having someone accuse Zeus of lying really made me mad. My power released and I began levitating in the air without even thinking about it. "Zeus is an honorable king, and you should not accuse such a man of lying without proof," I said as I floated closer to the Elves. "Do you believe this is a trick?" I asked as I folded my wings in so as not to hit anyone.

"Your power has grown," Selene gasped. "You have so much power."

"We believe," Alianna said as she smiled at me. "We apologize for any offense towards Zeus."

"Thank you," I said as I released my power and dropped to my feet on the floor. As soon as my feet hit the dizziness set in, and I started to fall forward, but Victor teleported to me and caught me.

"You must be careful," he whispered too low for anyone else to hear. "There is something not completely right with you."

"I'm just clumsy," I said loudly and growled a bit. "I was in wolf form for many years and dead not too long ago."

Victor teleported us back to the front and helped me sit down.

I sat and took a drink of water before smiling at Zeus. "Excuse my interruption, please continue."

Zeus nodded and turned back to everyone. "We have scheduled the battle for next month and Victor has been using his spies within his father's network to let him know. Now, how should we fight this battle?"

FIVE HOURS LATER, nothing had been decided, but almost everything had been argued. Ares and I had left as soon as the meeting was adjourned for the day and returned to our room.

Selene met us at our room with a somber expression on her face and asked, "What aren't you telling me?"

Ares and I exchanged a look of confusion and then Ares said, "We do not know what you mean."

Selene walked to me and took my hand, chanting a searching spell over my body to look for illnesses, spells or anything abnormal. She dropped my hand and then looked at Ares a moment with a startled expression. She asked Ares, "Why aren't you seeking treatment?"

"Treatment for what?" Ares asked, growing angry.

"Have you not noticed Chandra's...I mean Artemis' dizzy episodes and fevers?" she asked.

"Yes, but the healer treated them and put me on bed rest

saying it was nothing to worry about," I said, feeling fearful at what she was going to say.

Selene looked at me a moment and I could see sadness there. She sighed and said, "You are in good health. You and the baby are fine. Ares on the other hand needs to be treated for a small illness which is affecting you by his nearness and your bond. Ares, may I speak with you outside?"

"No secrets," I said with a scowl.

Selene smiled. "I must speak with him alone a moment to cast a spell. I do not want you near him while I do it."

Ares kissed my cheek and walked out the door with Selene beside him. I sat on the bed and growled. I hated secrets. Most of my time with Ares had been in the dark because they hadn't wanted to scare me and had kept so many things from me. I had to hope that Selene was being truthful and that she would tell me if anything serious was wrong. I could not lose Ares.

"Is there somewhere we can go to speak in private away from Chandra?" Selene asked me with a sad expression once outside of the room.

"Yes, follow me," I said suspiciously. I did not like the look on her face. And I really did not like the lie she had told Artemis about the illness I supposedly had.

We walked in silence down the hallways passed many Sidhe and several of my pack. I was confident that Selene would not harm me as she and I had a civil past and she and Koda used to date when he was in his early hundreds. I did keep my guard up just in case she tried anything funny though. I never trusted anyone completely, except for Artemis.

I knocked on the door to Zeus' office and opened it. Seeing no one inside, I waved Selene in and then shut the door behind us.

"I don't understand how you could see an illness that the healer could not," I said honestly to her. "I do not mean to insinuate your skills are flawed or insult you, but the healer never even looked at me."

Selene smiled. "Which is exactly why she doesn't know what is wrong. She is so focused on Artemis and why Artemis is sick that she did not think about the fact that you and Artemis are tied to each other and that your illness is affecting her."

"Are you sure that I am ill?" I asked.

I felt great. I felt like I could take on an entire army.

Selene closed her eyes and began whispering a spell to look at my body and everything going on with it. I felt tingly and wanted to rub my arms to rid them of the goosebumps covering them, but being an alpha meant not showing weakness, so I held perfectly still and kept my breathing even to keep her from noticing my discomfort.

Her eyes opened and she said, "It is worse than I had originally thought. This is Noctum, the black illness. It starts off slowly with just fevers and dizziness, and then builds until the infected can't get out of bed and can't eat or sleep. Seizures will begin and then, ultimately, death."

"Why am I not showing any symptoms?" I asked.

"This illness is created so that it affects the person closest to you, magically and nearest you, physically. What I mean is that it is affecting Artemis through your bond, but if Artemis were not here it would most likely show on Koda. If Koda were not here it would go to the next person linked to you, perhaps your father or mother. The illness does this so that you do not treat the correct person and the person, and the one it is affecting, die before you realize that it was always the stronger one who was sick. Thankfully, some of us know about it and can see the signs and have spells to confirm it."

I stared at her in utter shock and disbelief. Not only was I dying, but because of my bond, Artemis was as well. "How did I receive this?"

"Only one gives this cursed illness, Death."

I grabbed the chair nearest us and threw it into the wall to my right. "No! That bastard did this because I forced him to give me their souls. No. This cannot be."

My child would be born soon, and I would continue to hurt Artemis until this illness killed me and her. There had to be some way to fix this. Even if I had to send Artemis away or if I had to isolate myself, I would do it.

"Is there a cure?" I asked after calming down a moment.

"Yes," she said, but not cheerfully which meant that it was complicated.

I sat down in a chair and met her eyes. "What is it?"

"It's not easy and not a cure most would go through with."

"Tell me!" I commanded and then sighed. "I apologize."

"It's quite alright. I understand that you are worried for Artemis and your child due to this illness affecting them. It is understandable." She paused a moment and then said, "To cure Noctum one must perform the appropriate spell, which uses dragon's blood and a soul."

"A soul?" I gasped and then sighed. "A sacrifice. I would need Dragon's blood and a sacrifice."

"Yes," Selene said as she nodded. "The spell makes the being, and whoever they are tied to, practically immortal. There are many who would abuse the spell, such as Maurice. The spell was hidden from the world because of this and only the leaders of the witches know of the spell. I am willing to use this spell on you because I have known you a couple hundred years and know you will not abuse your immortality, especially not with Artemis by your side. I am sorry to be the bearer of such bad news, but Ch-Artemis is one of my sisters and her safety is of great concern to me. I will leave you and visit with your mate another day." She walked out of the office and closed the door behind her softly.

I slumped in the chair and ran a hand over my face. What was I going to do? I needed to get a cure before the illness affected Artemis and the baby any more, but Artemis was not going to take this well. I could hide it from her while I searched out an appropriate person to sacrifice, but knowing her, she would think the worst and panic and overreact. If I tried to send her away, she would just teleport back to me. And if I left, she would try to track me.

I did not particularly like the idea of sacrificing someone to keep myself alive. If it had been Artemis in danger, I would do it in a second. I could not leave my child now that I was finally going to have one. I had waited too long for this moment.

"Ares?" Mother said as she opened the door and entered the room. "What is wrong?"

"What?" I asked as I looked up at her.

She smiled. "I am your mother. I can sense your unease a mile away. What is troubling you?"

My mother, Beatrice, was a smart and level-headed person. Well, as level-headed as any female wolf could be. She was probably the best person for me to discuss the matter with to get help in making my decisions.

"I am having a dilemma and I am not sure how to deal with it," I said.

She sat down in a chair beside me and then noticed the chair embedded in the wall across the room. She smirked and said, "I see. Maybe I can help you."

I took a deep breath and said, "You must promise not to speak of it to Artemis or Koda."

Her eyes widened. "You have never kept secrets from your brother before. Is this so terrible that you must now?"

I nodded and she smiled. "Very well. I promise."

I described to her in detail what had happened in Death's realm and every word Selene had said. Mother listened passively and stayed silent a long time after I was done, mulling everything over in her head as she weighed out the choices. She had been a good Queen and had had to make many hard decisions. "I am not sure what your dilemma is, to be honest. Are you just unsure as to who to pick for your sacrifice?"

That was the woman I knew. Sure of right and wrong and capable of making choices that others might cringe at if it would ensure the safety of her pack.

"I am worried about how Artemis will react and yes, I am unsure of who to choose."

"Does your conscience really worry about picking someone to die for you? For your child? I would think you would go out and snatch up the nearest being from the cells and snap his neck right away if that would do it."

I smiled. "Normally, that would be my reaction, but it is not the child's life on the line. My life is the one on the line."

"Artemis is a strong woman and might make it through your death, but then again she might not. She did just lose the man she was bound to. I'm not sure if she could handle her *passt genau* dying as well."

I had already thought the same thing, but didn't want to admit the weakness in Artemis.

"Plus, Selene said that both of you would die and if she died before giving birth, that would mean the death of your child as well. I can have a list made of potential sacrifices if you would like? I will go and personally handpick the person to be sacrificed. I do not want to see another one of my son's bodies lying before me. You are supposed to far outlive me, not the other way around," she said seriously.

"A list would be helpful," I admitted. Though the slight nagging on my conscience would not go away. It was one thing to kill to protect someone or yourself but using someone for a spell was not something I was used to. I did see her point about saving Artemis and our child though.

"Are there restrictions on what type of being it is? Or their health?" Victor asked from beside me.

I had felt him appear a second earlier but had not acknowledged him. Mother growled at being scared by his sudden appearance, plus she had never liked him anyways.

"I don't know," I said with a shrug. "I did not ask Selene."

He paced across the room with a cloud of black hanging around him. It was rare to see the vampire in such a state of worry. "We need to ask her. If we could find someone who had a serious illness and wanted to die soon then your conscience would be eased with using them."

I smiled at Victor. My oldest friend knew me better than most.

The door flung open and Artemis rushed to me. "What happened? What did Selene say?"

I pulled her onto my lap and held her against my chest. She was warm again and shaking slightly. "You were supposed to stay in bed," I said with no real anger in my voice as I was happy to touch her and smell her.

"Don't change the subject," she murmured as she buried her nose into the side of my neck, inhaling my scent for reassurance and to help her calm down.

"The symptoms you are having are actually Ares'," Mother said. "He is dying and if you stay near him then you will die as well." So much for her not speaking of it to Artemis.

Artemis stilled, her heartbeat slowing with the lack of breath. "No," she whispered after a moment, "Selene has to be wrong."

"There is a cure," Victor said as Artemis' fear began to build.

"What is it? Why aren't we working on it now? Is that where Selene is? I can go help her and..." she stood up and then her legs gave out.

I caught her easily and pulled her back on my lap. "Easy, Sunshine."

"Victor and I will go speak to the witch. We will get this started now," Mother said as she motioned for Victor to follow her.

Artemis grabbed my face between her hands and forced me to meet her pale face. "I can't lose you. I can't. I am not strong enough to deal with your death."

I kissed her nose softly and smiled. "You won't lose me. However, you are losing the use of your legs because I am now forbidding you from walking anywhere for the next twenty-four hours." I picked her up and carried her down the hall to our room.

"What needs to be gathered for the spell?" she asked.

I clenched my teeth, not wanting to discuss it with her. I had forgotten for a moment that she had been Chandra for a long time and that she was well acquainted with the steps needed to perform spells.

"There are a couple items which Victor and my mother will work on gathering. You do not need to worry about it."

"Of course, I'm worried," she said with a sob. "Why is there always so much death around me?"

I kissed her head and set her down on the bed. "This is not your fault, Artemis. I have not led a very virtuous life."

"Tell me what needs to be collected for the spell," she said in her best alpha voice.

It was a good tone, one that would make lower dominance wolves bow in submission. I was impressed.

"Dragon's blood and a sacrifice," I said softly.

"A sacrifice. Why does it have to be a sacrifice? The dragon's blood I could get easily, but a sacrifice will be harder to find," she whispered. She tapped her chin a moment and then snapped her fingers. "I know! We will just go to the dungeons and take the worst criminal there and use them."

"I had already thought of that," I said with a smile. "I just don't particularly like the idea of someone being killed for me. If it were a battle and I had to kill or be killed then it would be an easy choice, but this is not a battle."

She turned my face to meet her gaze. "You listen to me. I will get you cured. I will not let you die. Maybe there is a way around the sacrifice. I will not let this illness hurt our child either."

I smiled and kissed her cheek. She was learning too much from me. She was right about one thing though. I could not let my illness harm our child. I had to stop being cowardly and be an alpha and a father. I had to choose a sacrifice.

"Ares?" Koda called through the door. "May I enter?"

"Yes."

Koda entered and immediately rushed over to Artemis. "What happened? I felt your fear and rushed here."

"Protect Artemis, I'm going to speak to Zeus," I said as I pulled out of her hold.

Artemis grabbed my arm. "Ares—"

I kissed her cheek. "You cannot stop me from protecting you and our child."

"Let me contact Draco Blu first. Maybe the Dragon Council knows of a different way. One that doesn't include a sacrifice," she pleaded.

"Sacrifice? What the hell is going on?" Koda asked.

"Artemis will explain while I am away. Keep her on the bed and do not let anyone inside and do not let her walk," I ordered him. I pulled away from Artemis and walked out the door to find my father.

ELEVEN

"Artemis, what is going on?" Koda asked. "Why does Ares need a sacrifice?"

I sat down on the bed and cried, unable to hold it in any longer. "Ares is dying," I croaked out between sobs.

"What?" Koda bellowed. "How?"

"Death's way of getting one over on Ares for getting my soul back. He cursed Ares with Noctum, the black illness."

"Is there a cure?" he asked.

I wiped my eyes, trying to calm myself down and recompose myself into the leader that I was. "Yes, but it requires a sacrifice."

"Done," he said seriously. "I will sacrifice myself."

I wanted to slap him. "No!" I screamed. "You are not dying! We need you."

"Darlin' you don't need me. As long as you have Ares, that's all that matters. Besides, if I can ensure he will live then I would gladly give my life."

"Koda stop it. You are not dying," I snarled.

"Alright, calm down," he said, but I knew he wasn't being completely honest with me.

I rolled onto my side and put my head in his lap. "I can't live without you."

"That's sweet, Darlin', but the only one you can't live without is Ares. I'm just your packmate."

"Stop it," I ordered him.

He stroked my hair and whispered, "I missed you so much those hundred years. And when you died, it tore a piece of my heart out. I thought I would never feel whole again and then you came back and I had never been so happy in my life. I realized then that even though I can never have you as my mate and you will never love me like you do Ares, I could at least be happy knowing you're alive."

I sat up and stared at Koda. "What are you saying? That you love me?" I asked him. He had never spoken to me in such a way before.

"Yes," he said seriously, "but I do not expect you to say anything or even acknowledge my feelings for you. It is enough for me that I am in your life."

"Does Ares know?" I asked, still reeling from this news. How could he say such things?

"I assume he does, but we have not discussed it. Do you understand now why I would sacrifice myself for Ares and you? To save either of you from death would be the greatest death for me," he whispered.

"I order you to stop," I said to him. "You are not going to die. No one is going to die!" Tears were streaming down my face and I couldn't see. Why was this happening? Why did everyone have to die around me?

"Alright, easy," he whispered as he pulled me closer to him. "Let's drop the subject."

"I can't let anyone else die. Never again," I whispered. A plan formulated in my head and I knew it would work. I only had to convince Ares and Zeus to allow it.

THE NEXT DAY the meeting was called again. I sat down and listened as they argued for an hour and held my tongue, but as nothing was accomplished still, I raised my hand, and everyone turned to stare at me. "I have information regarding Maurice's plan and another bit of information that I feel everyone here must know."

"What information? Where did you acquire this information?" Zeus asked. I knew he wasn't trying to be rude to me, he was just exasperated with the situation of everyone arguing in circles.

"When I was grieving over Achilles, I allowed myself to be captured by the vampires. They took me to Maurice, and I used my ability to create sunlight and surrounded him and all of the vampires in the room in sunlight. All of his vampires died instantly, but he didn't," I said.

"He is resistant to sunlight?" Victor gasped. "I never knew. He wasn't born and never went into the sun, so I assumed he could not."

I nodded. "He sat in the sunlight with no pain whatsoever. He is in fact able to walk in sunlight."

"We are doomed! How will we defeat him?" one of the trolls asked.

I waited until the room was quiet again and said, "He is still vulnerable to fire."

"So, why didn't you use fire?" Alianna asked.

I smiled. "I did, but he escaped, and I was too weak to pursue him. I returned back to Ares after that."

"What is the information you have about his plan?" Ares asked. I could see he was irritated that I had not mentioned it to him before, but I had been a little preoccupied with finding out about his death.

"I have a plan that I believe will ensure the demise of his reign. It will take a lot of coordination and will require you all to trust me, but if we do this, I am sure we will win."

"Is it suicidal?" Ares asked.

I sighed in exasperation. "No."

"Has anyone contacted Draco Blu since the funeral?" I asked.

"No," Zeus said, "The dragons have always preferred to be neutral, so we did not contact them to discuss our battle."

"I'll contact him tomorrow," I said, "I am sure that they will come when I tell him of the news."

"What news?" Hera asked.

"I would prefer to reveal it to all of the races at once. I do not wish to cause undue alarm. I would ask that we reconvene tomorrow morning and I will reveal everything then and we can begin to arrange our attack."

Zeus tapped his chin. "Agreed. We will reconvene tomorrow at eight in the morning."

I stood and Ares linked hands with me, walked beside me as we headed out of the room and to our chambers. "You seem different," he said softly as we walked.

I smiled up at him. "I am just remembering that I am not a little girl anymore. I am over one hundred years old and I am the leader of the werewolves just the same as you are. I have to start acting like the alpha that I am."

He wrapped his arm around my waist and whispered into my ear, "I like it when you talk like an alpha."

I laughed and pulled away from him when we got to our chambers. "As soon as Victor pops in I will tell you what I learned since I know you will pester me until I tell you."

"I do not pester people," Ares said indignantly, "I order them, and they surrender and grovel at my feet."

I rolled my eyes at him. "I am not going to gravel at your feet."

Amber flickered over his eyes and he said, "That would be a very fun thing to see though. Perhaps I should give you an order as your alpha."

I smirked at him and backed up towards one of the chairs in the room. "You could try."

I started to sit, and Victor said, "While I do find our friendship has grown, I had not known it had moved to the point where you would sit in my lap."

I growled and spun around, sitting in the chair opposite him. "I hate when you do that."

He smiled. "Ah, but I do love the shock it gives people."

"Hopefully he gets over it within the next hundred years," Ares said.

"So," Victor said, drawing us back to the topic at hand, "What news do you have? You have guarded your mind so well with thoughts of unicorns and kittens that I have not been able to discern it."

"Unicorns and kittens?" Ares asked.

I shrugged. "I had to figure out a way to keep him from hearing my thoughts and I figured he would grow bored of me thinking about those animals."

"Well played," Victor said, "Although I did see that whatever it is will cause widespread panic across the world."

Ares sat down in the chair beside Victor and I took a deep breath and began. "Your father believed that I was permanently in his hold so he thought it was okay to divulge his strategy to me because there was no way I could get the information back to Ares and let him know. Maurice has stationed vampires all around the world in anticipation of our group attacking him. When we lead our attack, he will signal his vampires who will attack all of the defenseless beings who were left behind. They will march into Lyngvi for example and his vampires will kill every female, child, and submissive male that has been left there."

Ares growled and began pacing around the room. Victor linked his hands together and rested his chin on top of them with his elbows resting on the arms of his chair. "It's a brilliant plan."

"Even more brilliant now that we know," Ares said in a deep growl.

"How so?" I asked.

"Now that we know what he is planning, we will have to split up our attack force. Instead of all of our strongest attacking him, we will have to send some of each to protect our weakest. He has successfully separated us and diminished our force," Victor said. He looked at me a moment and then said, "But you have a plan for that." I smiled and started thinking about a kitten riding a unicorn. He scoffed. "Think about all the kittens and unicorns you want. I will wait until tomorrow to hear your plan." He stood up and bowed to me. "Goodbye, *Mon Papillion*."

He disappeared and Ares plopped down into the chair he had just vacated. "You have a plan?"

I nodded.

"Are you going to tell me it?" he asked.

I shook my head.

He sighed. "I am your mate and you will not tell me your plan?"

I smiled and said, "I have a plan and I will reveal it and these details to everyone." Something moved inside of my stomach and I looked down at it in shock. "What was that?"

Ares walked over to me and rested his hand on my stomach. "Did the baby kick?"

I shrugged. "I don't know. It felt like a weird bump." I looked at my stomach, which was noticeably larger now. When had my stomach expanded so much?

He titled his head to the side and placed his ear to my stomach. The strange feeling happened again, and Ares smiled. "The baby's kicking."

I smiled and rested my hand on top of Ares' head. "In order for my plan to work, we will have to wait until after I have our child."

Ares lifted his head up and rested his chin on my stomach so that he could look at me. "Why do I get the feeling that I am not going to like this plan?"

I leaned forward and kissed his forehead. "You are a very perceptive man."

He growled. "You are infuriating."

I closed my eyes and felt exhausted. Would we be able to cure Ares before I had our child? "Am I going to have stretch marks?" I asked him with my eyes still closed.

He laughed softly. "Yes, but they will heal almost instantly. After you have the baby your body will repair itself quickly."

"I'm scared," I whispered.

He moved and before I could inhale, we were lying on the bed and he was cuddling with me underneath the blankets. "I will do everything that I can to keep you safe."

I nuzzled his throat and intertwined our legs together. "I'm not scared because of that. I'm scared of childbirth."

"Speak to my mother. She can talk with you about it and ease your fears," he whispered.

I kissed his neck and then settled against him. "Sometimes I wish we could pause the world and simply live in moments like this."

"So do I," he whispered.

"Ares?" Koda called through the closed door. "Has Artemis eaten yet?"

"No," Ares said, "Please get her something and me as well."

We heard Koda's footsteps walk away and only after I was sure that he was gone did I relax against Ares again. I dozed in his arms until Koda returned and then tried to eat despite the nausea which had decided to return as soon as I sat up.

"Get Selene," Ares whispered to Koda when he thought that I was not paying attention.

"She is at the door," Victor said from the chair beside me.

I lifted my head to look at him and immediately regretted it. Victor grabbed me and a moment later set me on the floor of the bathroom with my head over the toilet and my hair pulled back in his hands.

"*Thank you,*" I thought as I threw up everything that I had just eaten.

"You're welcome."

Ares came into the bathroom and took Victor's place holding my hair. "Selene is here, and she has good news."

I took a deep breath and forced my stomach to stop squeezing its contents out. I hoped this was not going to be a constant thing. After being sure that I was done throwing up I sighed, and Ares picked me up and carried me out to the bed.

Selene placed her hand on my forehead and chanted a fever

reduction spell and then made me drink a disgusting tasting anti-nausea potion. "Better?" she asked. I nodded and she sat down beside me on the bed. "I spoke with Draco Blu yesterday. He and two thirds of his flight will be joining our battle against Maurice."

"That's great," I said with a smile. Having the dragons would be a huge advantage for us because of the fire they produced in an endless quantity.

"And," she continued, pulling a chain from underneath her shirt which lifted a vial that was attached to it, "he gave me this."

The vial had green liquid inside of it that glowed softly.

Ares walked towards us and Selene placed the vial and necklace in his hand. "Is this dragon's blood?" he asked.

She smiled and eyed the vial. "It is Draco Blu's blood to be precise."

"The Draco of the dragons gave you his blood?" Victor asked, furrowing his brow.

I smiled and felt extremely grateful for the friendship that I had created with him. He had given me many gifts and had protected me many times when I was Chandra. I would need to find a way to repay the large debt I now owed him. It would not be easy, but it was necessary.

Selene said, "She was the favored hatchling of Draco Blu and his flight. It is a very rare honor."

"She is very good at getting people to like her," Victor said.

I wasn't sure what he meant by that, but I did not think he meant any disrespect, so I let the comment lie. "Have you chosen a sacrifice yet?" I asked Ares.

He shook his head and Victor said, "We have one chosen for him."

"Who?" Ares asked, obviously not happy with that news.

"A prisoner who was sentenced to be put to death, but whose sentence has yet to be carried out. He committed violent crimes that are unforgivable and as such there is no reason why he should not be used for a sacrifice."

"Will the death be painful?" Ares asked Selene.

Selene glanced at me and I knew as well as she did that sometimes sacrifices in spells were very painful. Often times the person would scream for the duration of the spell. "It will be painful but will not last more than two minutes."

Ares did not look reassured by that answer. "I will pick the sacrifice myself."

"You had better choose in the next day or two," Selene warned. "Artemis is getting worse and the baby is beginning to suffer."

My hand instinctively went to my stomach and I felt fearful for my unborn child. Ares set the vial of Blu's blood in my hand and walked towards the door. "Victor, would you please protect Artemis for a few hours?"

"Of course," Victor said and then stood up.

Ares shut the door behind him, and I gaped at it. "What just happened?"

Selene stood up and smiled at me. "I will come see you tomorrow. We should be able to perform the spell then."

She left and I looked at Victor who was frowning. "What just happened?" I asked again.

"Ares went to blow of some steam and then to find someone suitable for the sacrifice. Now that he knows the baby is in danger, he will not hesitate in picking someone. Don't worry. He will be back soon."

I laid down on the bed and asked, "Why is he being so stubborn about choosing a sacrifice?" I really did not understand it. I would have chosen someone as soon as I found out about it if I had been able to.

"He does not like the idea of picking someone to die in his place. It is different when that person is attacking you and it is either them or you then it is to choose someone to be used in a spell. Many consider using a sacrifice to be a dark art and stay away from it."

"Selene told him already that I would die as well as him and so would the baby. So why is he now going? Why has he been putting it off?" I frowned.

"I understand your frustration, but Ares is very old and is very set in his ways. He is not used to not being in control. He is used to taking care of everything himself, but now he cannot. He is upset because you constantly put yourself in danger and he is upset that you and your child are in danger and he is upset that he cannot rip off Death's head in order to fix it all."

"Artemis?" a soft male voice asked from outside my door. "Can I come in?"

"Who?" I started to ask.

Victor whispered, "Apollo. I do not think Ares would like it if…"

"Come in," I called, not letting Victor finish.

Victor sighed. "Ares is going to have a brain aneurism when he learns that I let him in here with you."

I smiled. "You'll protect me if I need it."

Victor rolled his eyes. "Don't patronize me, Artemis. I am over a thousand years old."

Apollo walked into the room and I was awestruck again by how similar we looked. His hair was incredibly blonde now though. It looked almost magical. "Hello, Apollo," I said as I sat up. He was wearing blue jeans and a white t-shirt. He was a halfbreed like me so didn't that mean that he could switch to a wolf form?

Victor set pillows behind me so that I was propped up and discreetly shook his head at me. "What business do you have with Queen Artemis?" he asked Apollo when he turned around to face him.

"I heard that you were not feeling well," he said as he walked closer to the bed.

"Just a slight side effect to being pregnant," I said with a smile.

He smiled back at me. "You lie very poorly."

Victor stepped between Apollo and the bed and said, "That is close enough."

"Is he your bodyguard?" Apollo asked me. "I thought they said you were the prince or something?"

"He is a friend and yes, he is the Prince of Vampires," I said before Victor decided to show him how strong he was.

"You have a lot of friends," Apollo said. He sat down in one of the chairs in front of the bed and said, "I came to apologize to you."

"Now is not the time for your apology," Victor hissed.

"Victor, it's alright." I hated that everyone was babying me.

"No, he is right," Apollo said. "When you are feeling better and your mate is back then I will come visit you again."

"Apollo," I called, stopping him. He turned around and faced me, waiting for me to talk. "Why did you surrender after the battle?"

"Another time," he said with a shake of his head. "We will talk about that at a later time."

"Thank you for coming to see me," I said with a smile.

He smiled back. "I am glad that you are alive. I felt...

strange when you died, and I did not like it." He frowned at what he had said and left without another word.

"I do not trust him," Victor said.

"He saved me from my father and killed him for me. I trust him." Plus, Achilles had told me to make amends with him and I would.

"Artemis, it was not…" Victor started, but I glared at him and he stopped talking, raising his hands in surrender. "Alright."

Koda came into the room with his mother behind him. She smiled at me and hurried over to put her hand on my stomach and whisper to the baby. It was strange, but I was not about to disrespect her by telling her I thought she was weird. Victor smiled and then sat down in one of the chairs to relax.

She stood up and asked, "How are you feeling?"

"Same," I lied.

She tsked at me. "You cannot lie to me sweetheart. I am older than even Ares."

"I'm scared," I admitted. "I'm scared because the baby is beginning to suffer according to Selene. I'm scared because my stomach is expanding very very quickly, and I am scared because I have never had a baby and I'm afraid of what it is going to be like." Tears filled my eyes and I wiped them away, hating that my emotions were getting the better of me.

She sat down on the bed beside me and put her arm around my shoulders. "It is alright to be scared sometimes. I was scared when I had Ares. I was terrified that Hera would try to kill him. I was even scared when I had Matt and Koda because I was huge with twins."

"Will it hurt?" I asked her.

She gave me a kind smile. "Yes, but you will survive. Our deliveries are usually very quick and although they are painful, our bodies repair the damage right away. You will be exhausted for the first couple of hours afterwards, but then you will be good as new."

"Will the stretch marks heal?" I asked softly.

She laughed. "Yes, child. You will look like it never happened."

I exhaled in relief and rubbed my stomach. "We haven't even picked a name yet."

"I believe the healer will be coming today to tell you the gender. I would wait until Ares is here though," Koda said.

Of course, I would wait for Ares. Why did he think I would do something so rude?

"Where is my eldest?"

"Seeking out a sacrifice," Victor said from his chair.

"Good," she said as she stood up. "It is about time he took charge of this."

I laid down again and closed my eyes. "Why am I so tired?"

"You are growing a being inside of your body," she said. "It takes up a lot of your nutrients and energy. In fact, Koda, would you get us some food?"

"Yes, ma'am," he said with a bow of his head and left the room.

Beatrice looked at Victor. "May I have some privacy to speak with my daughter-in-law?"

Victor frowned. "Normally I would leave, but Ares asked me to protect her."

"I am not going to hurt her," she said, narrowing her eyes at him.

Victor shrugged. "I don't know that for sure. Besides, I would rather not leave her alone with anyone but Ares. She is very vulnerable right now and needs as much protection as possible."

"And you think that I would not be able to protect her? You forget that I am older than even you, Victor of the Vampires. I could be Alpha still, if I so desired."

"I do not doubt your strength. I am simply refusing to leave Artemis without me as an additional defense," he said adamantly. I had never seen him so serious about anything before.

She glared at him, but finally relinquished and turned to me. "The mind reading vampire already knows this so I might as well discuss it in front of him. Have you talked with Ares about Koda's feelings for you?"

"I only found out about his feelings yesterday," I said uncomfortably. Was it just obvious to everyone that he had feelings for me, or had he talked to his mother about it? Which was worse? "And I did not think it was a good idea to bring it up to Ares due to his recent mood."

She sighed. "My sons have mostly gotten along, but I fear this might ruin the bond they had formed. Koda looks up to Ares and loves him like any younger brother should, but his feelings for you have only escalated since your disappearance and then death."

"He told me that it was enough just to be in my life," I said. "I'm hoping that he keeps that mentality."

"He might for a while," she said, "But his jealousy might also grow and…" She stopped talking and then the door opened as Koda entered with food.

He smiled at me and set a tray of food on the bed beside me with a glass of water. "Sorry it took so long. I got side-tracked on my way to the kitchen."

"Thank you," I said and then picked up some food and started eating.

"You have always been the politest of my sons," she said with a smile at Koda.

He took a seat in a chair next to Victor and then sat very still. It was weird looking, and I was about to ask what he was doing when Ares flung open the door and charged inside. "Why do I smell Apollo?"

He was seething with anger and I could almost see a red cloud encircling him. "Ares, what's wrong?" I asked as I stood and started towards him.

"Get in bed," he said. "Stop moving around," he growled. He had never growled at me or been seriously mad at me before. I continued walking towards him and he growled again. "I order you to get in bed," he snapped, his order as alpha pressed against me like a net pulling me backwards.

I growled back at him and held my ground, trying my hardest to slide my feet forward.

"Stop, Ares. You're going to hurt her," his mother said.

"I wouldn't be hurting her if she would obey," he said. "For once in your life, obey."

"Come here, Ares," I ordered him in my best alpha voice and using as much of my dominance as I could.

His body jerked towards me and his eyes widened. He apparently did not know that I could order him around just as he could me. He held his ground and gnashed his teeth together.

"Even if you prove your point," Victor said, "You will only feel bad about hurting her afterwards. We all agree that Artemis needs to start taking some orders."

"I just want to touch you," I said to Ares. He was being obstinate, but I was much better at it.

"Why was Apollo here?" he asked me again.

"He came to visit me," I said. "He wanted to check on me because he had heard that I was ill."

"Who let him in here?" Ares screamed.

He was getting too worked up and soon would let his bloodlust take over if he was not careful. I had never seen him in such a fit before. I had to do something, but what could I do to diffuse the situation?

"Victor," I said softly. "Teleport them out of here so I can speak to my mate alone."

"No one is going anywhere until I get answers," Ares said.

"I let him in," I said. "Victor was guarding me, so I was perfectly—"

"You let him in here with my sick mate?" Ares screamed at Victor as he walked towards him.

Victor stood and I could see the slight worry in his eyes and the tension in his body. "Artemis allowed him in and I stood between him and her and forced him to keep his distance from her. She was not in serious danger."

Victor was the only one who saw the punch coming because he turned to mist, and Ares' fist went through him.

"Ares," I yelled. "Stop it!"

Victor drifted away and reformed across the room. "I know you are upset, but you do not want to fight me."

Ares shifted into warrior form and charged Victor. Koda tried to grab him, but Ares flung him across the room. Koda spun at the last second, bouncing off the wall with his feet instead of slamming into it. He ran forward and kicked Ares in the back of the knees, making him stumble as he lunged at Victor who was teleporting around the room trying to stay out of his reach.

"Ares, calm down," Victor said in a soft voice. "I understand that you are stressed out, but you do not want to hurt me."

Ares roared at Victor--logical thought gone as he tried to attack him. Koda jumped onto Ares' back and tried to wrap his arm around Ares' throat, but Ares simply grabbed Koda by his arm and tossed him across the room, straight into Victor who thankfully misted before Koda hit him.

"Ares," Beatrice said. "Calm down, son." He turned and growled at her and she took a step back, fear emanating from her. I wondered why she was so afraid when she was older than him.

I approached Ares and set my hand on his forearm. He jerked away and spun towards me, ready to attack me until he saw my face. He lowered the hand he had raised at me and instead snarled at me. I took his clawed hand and gently set it against my face. His hand flexed and the claws bit into my skin just enough to draw blood.

Koda growled, and Ares started to turn towards him, but I grabbed Ares' other hand and set it on my stomach where the baby was kicking up a storm. He looked down at my stomach and his lips lowered, closing over his teeth and his body slowly started to return to his human form.

"Everyone out," I whispered.

Koda started to protest, but Victor grabbed him and teleported before he could move.

"I hope you know what you're doing," Beatrice whispered.

"Mate," I whispered, drawing Ares' attention back to me and away from his mother as she walked slowly out of the room.

He looked up at my face and growled. "Mate."

I took a step backwards, towards the bed, holding onto his

wrists and keeping them on my face and stomach. "Artemis," I whispered, hoping that he could slowly regain his control.

"Artemis," he whispered back as he looked down at my stomach from another of the baby's kicks.

"Baby," I whispered. "Your baby."

"My baby?" he asked.

I nodded and sat down on the edge of the bed, keeping his hand on my face. "Your baby. Your mate. Artemis."

The gold melted out of his eyes and he plopped face first down onto the bed on his stomach. "Artemis. Sorry."

I kissed his cheek and wrapped myself up in his arms and whispered, "Sleep."

He nodded, and we fell asleep together.

TWELVE

I woke up the next morning alone. *Completely* alone. I got out of bed, changed and peeked my head out the door. The hallway was empty too. "Hello?" I called, but only received my echo back. I walked down the hallway, running my hand along the wall in case I had a dizzy spell to keep from injuring myself and made my way out of the castle. I looked in each room that I went past, but all of them were empty, which was very strange considering that there were usually servants running around everywhere. Where was everyone?

I pinched myself and growled at the pain. I was definitely awake. My stomach grumbled, and I sighed. I was definitely hungry.

"Victor!" I called, hoping he would be listening or would be nearby. "Victor, where are you?" He did not appear in front or behind me, so I continued towards the front doors. I pushed them open, straining with the weight a moment. The doors opened and bright sunlight blinded me. I blinked my eyes until I could finally see and felt my heart drop at the sight before me.

Hundreds of beings were gathered in a circle in the field in front of the castle where Ares and Koda were standing in the center facing each other. I saw elves, wolves, Sidhe, halfbreeds and even a couple of dwarves and ogres standing in a circle around them, waiting. Koda was shirtless and judging by the amount of amber in his eyes, very angry. Victor was standing between Ares and Koda, talking quietly and quickly. No doubt he was trying to calm them down and talk sense into them.

"Victor," I whispered urgently.

He looked towards me and his eyes widened. He said something to Ares and then Victor teleported to me and picked me up. "Why are you out of bed and walking around?"

"I was alone," I said, "I'm never alone so I was worried. What is going on?"

He teleported so that he was standing between Koda and Ares again. "Koda, Artemis is here."

Ares reached to take me from Victor, but Koda growled at him and swatted his arms away from me. "You do not deserve to touch her."

"Set me down," I ordered Victor. He obeyed but gave me an irritated look so I apologized silently. "Koda, what is going on?"

He pointed at Ares and said, "He hurt you yesterday. He does not deserve to have you as his mate."

"Do not do anything that you will regret, brother," Ares warned him.

"Koda, he was experiencing bloodlust. It happens to even the best wolves. You cannot blame Ares for losing control once in over a couple hundred years. He has a lot on his plate right now and—"

"It is inexcusable that he hurt you," Koda roared, cutting me off mid-sentence.

"I am not hurt," I said, "It is not his fault—"

"He cut your face with his claws," Koda roared again. "I challenge—"

I punched him in the stomach as hard as I could, making him gasp for breath and stop talking. "Shut up before you do something you will regret."

He got his breath back and whispered, "He is letting you die for him. He is going to kill you."

"I am not letting her die," Ares growled.

Koda stood up straight, pushed me to the side into Victor's arms, and then charged Ares. I tried to move towards them, but Victor held on to me and due to my weakened state, I was unable to break free.

Ares blocked Koda's punches and kicks but did not hit him back. "Stop this," Ares said. "Let's talk about this in private."

Koda growled and shifted into his warrior form. "I challenge you for the position of Alpha of the Werewolves."

"No!" I screamed. "Koda, don't do this. If you kill Ares, I will never forgive you. Do you hear me? If you take him away from me, I will kill you myself!"

"Listen to her, Koda. She isn't bluffing," Victor urged.

Ares stayed where he was, watching and waiting for Koda's decision. I could see the tension in his body as he waited and knew that if Koda attacked him that he would not hold back.

Koda turned to me with hurt in his eyes. Part of me felt bad for threatening him, but I knew he needed to hear how I felt. I loved him as a pack mate, but Ares was my mate and the man I loved unconditionally. I would never forgive anyone that took him from me. "Why do you want him when he treats you poorly?" he asked. "I would treat you like the queen that you are."

"I love him, Koda. He is my *passt genau*, my one true love and the father of my unborn child. He treats me well and you would see that if you were not blinded by your emotions. No one can replace him."

"Fine, a fight to yield for the position of alpha," he said.

"I will not be your mate," I told him sternly.

He growled. "I am not fighting to take you as my mate, Artemis. I am fighting to take his position as Alpha."

"Why?" I asked. "Why is it suddenly so important for you to be alpha?"

"Because I have lived in his shadow for too long. It is time that the world knows me for who I am, and the wolves have a leader that will lead them properly," Koda said.

"I accept your challenge to yield for Alpha of the Werewolves," Ares said.

"What are you doing?" Victor asked, releasing me and walking towards Ares.

I looked around at the crowd, hoping to find a Sidhe who was manipulating Koda like Achilles had done before.

"He wants to take over as alpha, so I am willing to let him try. If I do not accept his challenge it will make me look weak and now is not a time that I can appear weak," Ares said angrily. "He has wanted to do this since Artemis went missing and I will let him." Ares looked at Koda and said, "I will not hold back just because you are my brother. If we go forward with this challenge, I will fight you with all of my strength and power."

"I would have it no other way," Koda said.

"This is ridiculous," I said angrily.

"What's going on?" Theseus, Koda's son, asked as he walked up to us.

"Your father is challenging Ares to become Alpha of the Werewolves," I said, trying to portray how ludicrous it was and hope that he would talk some sense into his dad.

Theseus folded his arms across his chest and said, "I wondered how long it would take him to do this. I guess your health finally pushed Dad over the edge."

My jaw dropped to the ground. "Are you serious? Aren't you going to try to stop him?"

He put his arm around my shoulders and squeezed. "It'll be alright. Dad won't kill him."

I screamed in frustration and stepped away from the idiot brothers and said, "I refuse to watch this." I teleported to the dragon's hive, letting Victor know where I was heading. I knew Ares would be mad, but I was safer in the hive than anywhere else in the world. I popped into the hive, in the tent where I had slept while waiting for the dragons to help me unlock my memories and found it empty, thankfully. I stepped out of the tent to be met by the Dragon Council.

"Greetings, Artemis Lupine," they said in unison.

I bowed to them as well as I could with my enlarged stomach. "Greetings, Council."

"What do we owe the pleasure of your company to?" they asked.

"Werewolf quarrels that I have no desire to witness. I came to see Blu, I mean Draco Blu, if he is available and to seek your counsel regarding some issues."

"Draco Blu has been missing for several days," the Council said. "We sent Fira to contact you, but due to your lack of knowledge we must assume he is now missing as well."

"Missing? What do you mean missing?" I asked in shock.

"We do not have the ability to speak telepathically over long distances," they said.

I paced back and forth in front of them nervously. "What could have happened? Do you think it is possible that he was taken hostage or killed?"

"All things are possible," they said.

I refrained from rolling my eyes and asked, "Did the dragons acquire any enemies recently?"

"No."

Could Maurice have found out that the dragons were going to assist us, and would he have been able to capture Blu, or kill him? I shuddered at the thought but could not believe that the dragon would be easily taken down. Fira was a smaller dragon, but almost as strong as Blu and not easily killed either.

"We had planned to send scouts, but…"

"But you did not want them to disappear as well," I finished for them. "I will investigate myself," I said, "It is the least I can do after everything the dragons have done for me."

"You should not travel alone in your condition," they said.

"If I return, my mate will not allow me to go search for Draco Blu. I cannot return there to find someone to go with me," I said as I resumed pacing.

"Then I will go with you," Victor said from behind me. I spun around, angry that the vampire had gotten the drop on me again. He bowed to the Council. "Greetings, Dragon Council."

"Greetings Victor, Prince of the Vampires," they said.

"I will accompany you while you search for the dragons so that you are protected and so that I can teleport you to a healer if your condition should worsen," he said to me.

"Are Ares and Koda alright?" I asked.

He shrugged. "They were still fighting when I teleported to check on you, per Ares' request."

Of course, he had sent Victor to check on me. "Fine, but just remember that I can teleport just like you can so if you teleport me away and I am not ready to leave, I will just teleport right back."

He smiled. "I know, Artemis." He turned to the Council and asked, "Can you give me the specifics of your last communications with the two dragons who are missing?"

"Draco Blu left three days ago to head for the Sidhe's ground opening. He usually contacts us by magical reflection once he has arrived at his destination to check on the status of the hive while he is away. This is not the first time that he has not contacted us, but it is very rare."

I knew the spell to speak by reflection and it was very easy. In fact, Blu and I had used it to communicate when he was away from me while I was with the witches.

"Would he be able to contact you if he was captured?" Victor asked as he began pacing back and forth in front of the Council.

"He should be able to find some way and that is the other reason we are worried."

"Has Fira contacted you since he left?" I asked.

"No."

My fear for the dragons grew, and I put out a hand to lean against Victor as I took deep, calming breaths. Victor said, "We will travel the path to the Sidhe's opening and look for any sign of a struggle and search for the dragons. We will report to you periodically."

"Thank you," the Council said.

"How are you feeling?" Victor asked me as he watched the dragons walk away.

"I actually feel a lot better than I have in a while," I admitted to him. "Perhaps it is because of the physical amount of distance between me and Ares."

He nodded his head. "Selene did mention that it would affect those closest to him. It may be a good thing that you are away from him for a while."

"How long will the battle between Koda and Ares last?" I asked nervously. I did not doubt that Ares would win, but I was nervous that he would get seriously hurt.

"Two or three days," he said.

"Days?" I gasped.

He nodded. "Koda is alpha material. I noticed it the day we went to rescue your little friend, Bret. If Ares were not around, Koda would be the logical choice for alpha. He is dominant enough and he has a leader's mind."

"Part of me does hope that he takes over as alpha," I admitted.

"Why?" Victor asked.

"Because then it would mean that Ares and I could relax and raise our child together in peace somewhere," I said longingly.

"You would still be the next in line for the Sidhe throne," he said.

"Do you really think Hera or Zeus are likely to die anytime soon?" I asked sarcastically.

He shrugged. "Stranger things have happened."

I thought of Achilles and his early death and turned away from Victor. Victor patted my back and said, "We should head out. I have a feeling that we are going to be in for a very long night."

"What if your father has them?" I asked him. "What can we do?"

"Let's deal with that later if it comes up. You need to start thinking positively."

I pushed my wings out of my back and flapped them, sending me up into the air. "Fine. Let's start looking. I am getting more worried about them the longer that we stand here."

Victor transformed into a bat and flew after me as we headed out of the mountain and towards the Sidhe mounds which were entrances to the Sidhe realm. The cold air blasted against us as we exited the mountain, and I was forced to squint my eyes against the snow and wind.

We flew and scanned the terrain below us. Halfway there. I began to get lightheaded and was forced to land, but I was happy to have not found anything yet. I sat on a log and looked at the forest around us. It was so quiet and peaceful and relaxing that I did not want to get up.

"It seems the closer we get to Ares, the worse your symptoms become. Perhaps it would be best if you returned to the Dragon's lair and stayed with them?" Victor suggested as he watched me from the tree he was leaning against.

How could he look so normal in a forest where he should seem so out of place? "I cannot sit on my hands and worry. I have to do something." Plus, me having idle time was not the best idea. I would think of the worst outcomes and freak myself out more than was necessary for the baby.

I stood up and walked towards Victor. "I never thanked you," I said to him.

"Thanked me for what?" He asked.

"You have been a great friend, Victor. Thank you for protecting Ares and staying beside him when I was away. I can't imagine what it must have been like to deal with him those hundred years that you were all searching for me."

He smiled. "Ares is my best friend. You do not need to thank me for anything."

The baby started kicking and I grabbed Victor's hand and placed it on my stomach. "Feel it?" I asked him.

He stared at my stomach with such awe and softness that it almost made me forget that he was a vampire and capable of as much, if not more, damage as Ares. "Such strong kicks," he whispered. "Does it hurt?"

I huffed. "No."

He pulled his hand away and smiled. "I am glad that Ares has you. He is a very lucky man."

I laughed. "*Right*. He is so lucky to have a troublemaker like me. I think I have caused him more headaches than he was expecting."

Victor smiled. "You may be right about that, but I saw him when you were stolen and again when you died and know that he would rather have you giving him headaches than you no longer in his life."

We made camp since it was so late and slept until the sun rose before heading out again. The day lagged on and still we found no trace of Draco Blu or Fira. I was just starting to lose hope when I inhaled to say something and smelled smoke. "Do you smell that?"

He nodded,and we both flew up into the air. I followed the scent of the smoke and gasped when we came to the scene. The forest abruptly ended in a ten-mile wasteland of ashes. There was no doubt in my mind that this was a scene of a dragon's fight. I hovered above the destruction and searched for any clues that might answer what the outcome of the battle had been.

"There are a lot of dead vampire ashes here," Victor called to me from the ground.

"How can you tell?" I asked him. To me the ashes looked the same as the burnt trees and bushes.

"I can tell," he whispered as he examined another streak of ashes.

I flew to the edges of the burnt forest, searching for signs of escape. Halfway around the damaged area I finally found marks, but the sight of them made my fear and worry skyrocket. Victor teleported to me and sighed when he saw the very large drag marks. He followed the marks and then returned to me. "They dragged him about a mile and then picked him up. He must be at my father's castle."

"Will he kill him?" I asked. And who was it? Was it Blu or Fira?

"No, he will not kill him. He will keep him prisoner to bait you into trying to rescue him and he will try to find ways to use him to his benefit," Victor said seriously.

My stomach clenched so hard that it made me gasp in pain. Victor grabbed me and said, "There is nothing we can do right now. We need to return and advise everyone what has happened."

"No," I said through gritted teeth.

"Hello, Victor," a deep voice said from behind us.

Victor did not turn around, but his entire body tensed up. Judging by his reaction, he had not heard the being arrive behind us. "Hello, Bartholomew," he said bitterly.

"I had expected Artemis to come in search of her dragon friends, but I had not expected you to be with her," Bartholomew said as he circled around to stand in front of us.

He was tall, dark and handsome. He was also very powerful and judging by his calm demeanor, not scared of Victor, which was not a good sign for us. I looked at Victor. *Is he susceptible to sun?* Victor shook his head.

"I came to assist her in her investigation," Victor said.

"Ah. You have always had a soft spot for the werewolves," Bartholomew said with a shake of his head. "Your heart is your biggest downfall."

"Would I be able to use fire on him without you getting burned as well?"

Victor laughed once and shook his head. "You only think that because you have no heart."

"Better to have no heart and be able to think clearly then to have a heart that clouds your thoughts and judgments."

"Where is the dragon?" I asked Bartholomew. The conversation between Victor and him was not going anywhere that would help us.

"He is with the king," he said, "Don't worry, you will be united with him soon, after I take you there."

"I have visited the King recently and I have no desire to go back to him so soon," I said with a smile. I turned to Victor. "What are we going to do?"

"First, Victor will die and then you will accompany me willingly to go see the king," Bartholomew said.

I rolled my eyes.

Victor smiled. "He has always been overly cocky. I think we have a couple of options, but I would prefer not to discuss them in front of Bart," Victor said as he moved a step closer to me.

I knew he wanted to teleport, and I knew that we probably should, but at the same time I did not want to return to Ares and have him force me to stay in the Sidhe realm. I needed to find Blu and Fira and I needed to do it quickly, before any harm came to them. I made up my mind and before Victor could say anything, I unleashed fire, covering Bartholomew.

He screamed and tried to turn to mist, but it did not

matter, I kept the fire on him until he was forced to fly away from us to save himself. Victor turned to me and laughed. "I cannot believe you made him retreat. That is the first time he has been forced to retreat in one hundred and eighty years."

I shrugged. "I needed him to leave and I did not want you to teleport us."

"Clearly," he said with a shake of his head.

"Alright, let's go. We need to find Blu and Fira," I said, taking a step towards the path of the drag marks.

Victor touched my arm, stopping me. "Let's not get ahead of ourselves. We should at least talk with Zeus…"

"No!" I yelled. "He will tell Ares and then I will be held captive. I have to do this without telling Ares. I thought we had already gone over this?"

"I know, Artemis, but if Bartholomew is involved then that means that all of the highest leveled vampires are involved. It is something too dangerous for just you and me to tackle," he said, grabbing my shoulders and forcing me to look at him so I could see how serious he was. "It is something that not even I should face alone. I will need the help of allies to face them."

"Then why don't you teleport and get Dmitri, Theseus, a couple other vampires still your allies and a couple other half-breeds if you think we need that many."

"And what are you going to do while I do that?" he asked me suspiciously.

I sat down, crossing my legs and said, "I will be right here."

He stared at me a moment and then asked, "What is the real reason that you do not want to return to the Sidhe realm?"

"I have been over this with you. I do not want Ares to keep me there."

"And?" he prodded.

I growled. "You can already read my mind so why are you asking me to say it out loud?" Vampires were so frustrating.

"Because you must say things out loud so that you make them real and realize your fears. It is not healthy to bottle things up."

"Do you pull this with Ares?" I asked him.

He smiled. "Yes, and that is one of the only reasons that he is sane right now."

"Fine, I will answer you. I am afraid to return to the Sidhe realm and to Ares' side because the closer I am to Ares the sicker I get. If I stay away from him the baby will not be in as much trouble."

He smiled. "Was that so hard?"

"You're an ass."

He laughed. "Alright, Artemis. I can tell that you are determined to go after the dragons so I will teleport and bring back enforcements. I do not like the idea of leaving you here, but I agree that it is better for the baby if we keep you farther away from Ares then he would normally let you be. You better be here when I get back."

I smiled. "I cross my heart." He rolled his eyes and then disappeared. I exhaled and rested my hand on top of my stomach. "What are we going to do little one? Your father is going to be extremely displeased with me for running away from him despite the fact that it is best for you. You will learn that he is very stubborn." I laughed. "But he is the greatest man I know. He will love you and you will be the greatest gift he has ever received."

Thinking about Ares made me think about the current predicament he and Koda were in. What would happen if Koda became the alpha? What would that mean for Ares and me? Would we be able to raise our child in peace while Koda helped the pack? The thought alone made a smile spread across my lips. A life where we could enjoy each other and spend time alone sounded mythical. I had to hope though. I had to keep hoping that someday it could happen.

Victor, Theseus and Dmitri popped into existence in front of me. Victor smiled and I smiled back. "You didn't think I would be here, did you?"

He laughed. "I have to admit that I assumed you would be on your way after the dragons already."

I stood up and said, "I'm trying to act mature. I believe a being over one hundred years old should start acting their age."

"Father and Ares are..." Theseus began.

I held up my hand, stopping him. "I do not want to hear about it. I will find out the result of their stupid fight when I return."

"Ares did ask about you when he saw me teleport in," Victor said.

"What did you tell him?" I asked.

Victor smiled. "I grabbed these two and teleported out without answering him. I did hear him roar before we left though."

"Good. He can deal with not knowing for a while."

"Shall we go?" Dmitri asked. "The night will fade soon."

I nodded, and Victor grabbed my hand, helping me stand. "I'm not that pregnant yet," I said teasingly.

He smiled. "No, but it is gentlemanly to assist a lady."

"So, did you wear one of those white curly powdered wigs back in the human time in Europe? The ones like the judges wore?" I asked him.

He walked next to me and said, "I did wear a peruke and I looked fantastic in it."

"He looked like a ninny," Dmitri said.

Victor rolled his eyes. "You did not look any manlier in knee length breeches and stockings."

"Can we please not focus on the fashion of such a dreadful time period?" Dmitri asked. "Can't we focus instead on the nineteen seventies? Those were wonderful years."

"That was a terrible time!" Victor exclaimed. "You have terrible taste in dress."

"Says the man wearing a puffy pirate shirt in the twenty-two hundreds," Dmitri said as he pointed at the shirt Victor was currently wearing.

I tried not to laugh, but I could not help it after the indignant look Victor gave Dmitri.

"Artemis," Apollo said behind me.

We all spun around and Victor moved in front of me in a protective stance.

"What are you doing here?" Victor hissed.

"I came to aid Artemis," he said.

"How did you locate us?" I asked him. "And how long have you been able to teleport?"

He shrugged. "I don't know. I just closed my eyes and focused on the tingle that tells me where you are and when I opened my eyes, I was behind you."

"Wait, you can locate me?" I asked him.

He nodded his head. "Don't you feel it? Can't you feel the tingle in the center of your head?"

Now that he mentioned it I could. I had just assumed it was part of the sickness of Ares' or because of the baby. I never imagined it was because he was my twin. "I never really thought about it," I answered softly.

"Go back," Victor commanded. "Ares is already fighting one person because of you."

"That is hardly fair." I frowned at Victor. "Apollo has done nothing to me since he surrendered and has tried to prove his desire to turn around from his previous life."

"He killed Achilles," Victor reminded me.

I turned my head away, fighting the emotions inside of me and the tears trying to leak out. "He did not know what he was doing. He had been brainwashed."

"Achilles would not so easily forget your death," Victor hissed.

I slapped him across the face before I thought better of it. "How dare you!" I screamed. "I have not forgotten Achilles' death. I ache from his loss every day but dwelling on the dead does not bring them back. Achilles came to me and told me to make amends with my brother and that is what I am trying to do."

"She slapped you," Dmitri whispered. "She actually hit you."

"I know," Victor said.

I wasn't sorry that I hit him, and I was not going to apologize for it just to calm him either. He had deserved that slap and he knew it. Victor laughed and shook his head. "I'm sorry, Artemis. Still, I cannot allow him to accompany us."

I groaned. "Why are you all so stubborn?"

"It's alright," Apollo said, "Just promise me that you'll be careful?" he asked softly.

I smiled. "I'm always careful."

Every one of them laughed at that, which I found incredibly rude. Apollo closed his eyes and disappeared. "Let's continue," Dmitri said.

I opened my mouth to say something to Victor, but he rested his hand on my shoulder and shook his head. "Let's forget it," he whispered, "I deserved your slap for being cruel."

The sound of a dragon screaming filled the night air from far away and instantly brought tears to my eyes. Without waiting for the others or even thinking about the possibilities of this being a trap, I flew up into the air and flapped my wings for all they were worth.

"Artemis, wait," Victor called.

"No," I said as I flew faster. "I will not abandon them in their time of need. I will rescue them. No one makes the dragons bleed. No one!"

THIRTEEN

I had hoped to shelter her from the fight that we would encounter when we found the dragons, but once she had heard the pain-filled scream of one, she would not be stopped. She flew ahead of us, her body glowing as she prepared to rescue one of the dragons whom she called friend.

It was still incredibly strange to me that the dragons and she were so fond of each other. Then again who was I to judge a strange friendship? Many had found Ares' and my friendship strange and unnatural and many still did. Perhaps I was too quick to judge others despite my attempts not to.

We raced through the wooded area, following the path they had created by dragging the dragon and the sound of the fight ahead of us. It was hard to keep up with Artemis, but I refused to leave her side since Ares was not here.

The sound of fighting grew louder and then we finally witnessed the chaos that was ensuing. Forty vampires were attacking Draco Blu and the dragon was holding his own, biting, clawing and decapitating vampires faster than the vampires could defend themselves. I took in the scene in less than a second, but it was already too slow because Artemis had joined in the fight. She grabbed a vampire, ripped him in half and then tossed the halves of his body into two other vampires, which allowed Draco Blu to grab them and bite their heads off. The two work easily together, never getting in the others way and seemed to anticipate the other's moves. It was incredible, and after two minutes, my presence was completely unnecessary.

Bartholomew ran from the shadows of the trees and leapt at Artemis, attempting to grab her. She saw him coming and teleported behind him. Bartholomew spun around and would have grabbed her if Draco Blu had not been there. Draco Blu grabbed Bartholomew with one of his giant Dragon's feet and slammed him into the ground, digging his claws into the dirt and pinning Bartholomew in place. Draco Blu growled at him and was about to engulf him in fire, but Artemis placed her hand on Draco Blu's shoulder and the dragon stilled.

"What is Maurice planning?" she asked Bartholomew, landing on the ground and folding in her wings so that she could stand and stare into his eyes.

"The King is planning on ridding this planet of the existence of werewolves and sidhe," he said.

"You don't have an army big enough for that," I said.

Bartholomew smiled and I did not like it at all. "Our plan is strong."

"You mean your plan to send vampires to kill the people who are not protected since all of the strongest warriors will be at the main battle?" Artemis asked.

Bartholomew's face scrunched in anger. "How did you know that?"

"Your king told me."

"No matter, we will still rule."

"Your plan will not work. We will kill any vampire who opposes us," she said looking as regal as ever.

She turned away from him and walked to the still body of a red dragon and knelt at its side. "Blu, you may dispose of the vampire however you wish."

"You need me," Bartholomew said.

"You killed my son. The only one who needs you is Death," Draco Blu said and then breathed fire onto Bartholomew until even his bones disintegrated.

Artemis wept as she lay across the dead dragon's neck. "I am sorry, Fira. I should have gotten to you sooner. I should have kept you all away from this."

Draco Blu lay down beside Artemis, wrapping his neck around her and his dead son and hummed a sorrowful tune. We watched them in silence, but after an hour Dmitri whispered, "The sun, Victor."

I rested my hand on his shoulder and teleported him and I to the darkened chambers he was sleeping in at Zeus' place and then teleported back to Artemis. When I returned she had stopped crying and was glowing as anger replaced her sadness. "Let's go get the egg back."

"We already got the dragon's egg back before you regained your memory," I reminded her.

"They took the Pegasus egg that I was bringing as a gift," Draco Blu said. "One of the vampires left the group as soon as they took it and returned to your King."

"If we go there now, we will be outnumbered and outmatched. We should wait for others to go with us," I pleaded.

Artemis looked at me and I had never seen her look so much like a Queen before. "Then we will return, and the war shall begin."

FOURTEEN

The battle between Ares and Koda was intense and very bloody. The ground around them was soaked in blood as they cut each other again and again, but their bodies healed the wounds and allowed them to continue on.

The audience had originally numbered in the thousands, but after two days of fighting it had dwindled to just their other pack members, Artemis' twin Apollo, and myself. I had seen Artemis teleport away the first day, which was probably for the best. The further away she was from Ares, the better she would feel and the more likely the baby and she would get healthy again. If it were up to me, I would send her and Ares to opposite sides of the world, but sadly it was not up to me.

The sounds of Koda and Ares' growls were the only noises in the Sidhe realm. It seemed that they were trying to be respectful, but part of me wondered how many of the Sidhe were hoping for Ares' loss, and even his death. They had agreed not to end this fight by death, but in the heat of the moment, things were known to happen, and more than one werewolf had died by the angry hands of another despite their prior agreement.

I doubted Koda would kill Ares, if he could, due to Artemis' declaration that if Koda killed Ares, she would kill Koda. I had seen the hurt in Koda's eyes, and like everyone, I knew that he loved her. How much pain was he enduring mentally as he fought his only remaining brother, knowing that if he killed him, the woman he loved would attempt to end his life?

I shook my head and sat down on the ground, smoothing out my dress as I did. Werewolf politics were always crazy, and it seemed even with Ares and Artemis in charge, that had not changed. I had already prepared my spell to use on Ares to cure him from Death's curse and I was certain I would not fail. I just prayed to the Goddess that we could perform the spell before Artemis and her child were affected too badly.

Koda and Ares backed away from each other and squatted down to rest for a moment. Koda's face was a mask of anger, while Ares' was stoic as usual when Artemis was not around.

Did he realize that his regal mask shattered the instant his mate was near him? I had known him hundreds of years, and it was good to see him so happy with a mate.

Two of Koda's sons walked out to Koda and Ares and gave them each one cup of water. Ares sipped it slowly, while Koda gulped it down. The brothers were not so different from each other really, but men refused to see the similarities in one another, especially when they loved the same woman.

Ares turned and looked at me, his eyes the molten gold of his wolf. "Artemis?" he asked in a clipped word. He was so tired and so frustrated that he could barely speak.

I shook my head. "Still gone."

He growled.

My hair rose at the predator's rumble. "She is safe. Victor, Dmitri, Theseus, and a couple others went after her to keep her safe."

He stood and growled again. Then he stretched out his body and regained control of his wolf. He stood straight and tall and even though his eyes were still his wolf's eyes, he was calm and collected once again. "Let's finish this so I can go find her."

"I would advise you to stay away from her," I said.

He turned and looked at me and I could see that his control was a hair's breadth away from slipping if he was pushed the wrong way. "Why?"

"The farther apart you are, the less sick she will be," I explained.

He growled. "I don't like being away from her or trusting others with her safety."

"You will like it less if your nearness causes her death," I admonished him with a scowl. I had grown attached to Artemis while she lived in the coven as Chandra. How I hadn't put two and two together was truly a mystery. Perhaps it had to do with Hera's spell? Or, I had just been blinded by the desire to protect Artemis like so many of these men were.

Ares growled and took a step towards me. I was only slightly afraid because I could incapacitate him long enough to get away and I knew he really did not want to hurt me. I did not have to do anything though, because Koda tackled Ares, taking advantage of his distracted opponent and not for the first time protecting me.

Seeing Koda's children had been hard, as I had fallen for the wolf at one time, but I'd let him go a century ago. Koda was a wonderful person, but we were not a good match.

The brothers attacked each other again and again and

despite my gnawing hunger, I stayed where I was. Artemis would ask for details, and I would be sure to have answers for her when she finally returned.

"Would you like some bread and cheese?" Zeus asked as he sat down beside me on the grass.

I took a piece of cheese and swallowed it whole before answering him. "Thank you. I am famished."

"I see not much has changed in their fight," he said, letting my rudeness slide without remark.

"Pretty much. They are both slower and more tired, but aside from that there has not been any progress," I reported. "And both are still in control of their wolves." Which was a very good thing. We did not need a rampaging werewolf on our hands, especially not one as strong as these two.

"Any sign of Artemis?" he asked with pinched eyebrows and a tight jaw.

"No, but I am sure she is fine. Victor and Theseus would never let anything happen to her," I assured him.

Zeus laughed and said, "I never expected the friendship between Ares and Victor to last so long. Most of us figured they would end up killing each other within the week, but thousands of years later their friendship is as strong as ever."

"The hatred between the races seems to have died out, especially in the last hundred years. It gives me hope that perhaps after we defeat Maurice, we will be able to unite all of the races and live peacefully," I whispered.

"That is the dream," Zeus said wistfully. We ate the food and watched the brothers fight in silence after that.

As the sun set, I prepared to nap a moment, but then Artemis appeared in front of me and sat down without even looking in my direction.

"Zeus, can you ask a servant to get me food?" she asked in a deep voice.

"They are already on their way to the kitchen," he said, moving closer to her.

"Stay back," she warned him. "Ares is losing control and I'm not at my best either. It would be better if everyone stayed a bit away, so we do not feel threatened."

"What happened?" I asked her.

"Vampires killed Fira and stole a Pegasus egg. We're leaving to start the war in three days."

"Ares and Koda will need time to heal," Zeus reminded her.

"They will be left behind then," she said coldly. "We don't have time to wait for them."

"I take it you have a plan," Zeus asked.

Why was he so calm and relaxed about her appearance and actions?

I wanted to drag her to her room and put her on bedrest as it was, but since she had told us to stay back, I assumed that meant her wolf was a bit too close for comfort.

She nodded. "Split up in teams. Save my Pegasus egg. Burn down any who oppose us."

"What about your baby?" I asked her, my eyes wide and shock almost palpable.

"He will be born tomorrow," she answered. "You will deliver him, and he will stay here in the Sidhe realm while we fight."

"What do you mean 'he'?" I asked, eyes wide.

"A mother knows," she whispered as she watched her mate and her packmate fight.

What must she be feeling, watching them battle?

"How do you know he is ready to be born tomorrow?" Zeus asked her.

Her eyes stayed glued to the fight as she continued answering us. "Victor told me the baby is ready. He said he wants out now."

"What?" Zeus and I gasped at the same time. I knew he could read minds, but how could he read a baby's mind?

She waved her hand dismissively. "Don't ask. It's not important. Just be ready to perform the spell and deliver my baby tomorrow."

"Why the sudden change in attitude?" I whispered to Zeus.

He shrugged and then whispered back, "It could be the dragon's death. She becomes emotionally attached to her companions, and it makes sense that she would become focused after an event like this."

I wasn't so sure, but I dared not question her when she was so close to the edge. I rose and headed to my chambers to prepare for the spell and prayed to the goddess that everything would go according to plan.

For once.

FIFTEEN

I switched forms while I slept and when I woke, I was still in my wolf form, lying on the grass outside.

Ares and Koda were still fighting which astonished me and angered me at the same time. I wanted to march out there and slap some sense into them, but I knew I could not interfere with the challenge and had to let them finish.

One of the Sidhe servants brought me out a plate of meat and set it down a few feet from me.

"Anything else, Princess?" she asked softly.

I shook my head and waited until she was gone before eating every last piece of meat and licking my paws and snout clean to get any traces left. The baby was making me very hungry and I was having cravings for sugar and meat, although those cravings were not altogether abnormal for me.

Ares and Koda separated to catch their breaths and Ares finally noticed me.

I locked eyes with him a moment and then turned my head away to show my disapproval.

"Artemis," he whispered, "are you alright?"

I turned around, flicking my tail at him and let him look at my butt as I laid down again with my head between my paws.

I can still communicate with you, even if you want to show me your cute butt.

I sighed, really hating werewolf telepathy. *Hurry up and finish your fight. Our child is going to be born today.*

"What?" he asked out loud instead of telepathically.

"What's wrong?" Koda asked.

"She said the baby is going to be born today," Ares answered.

"Then I will stop toying with you and end this." I heard Koda slam into Ares and I cringed, thankful that he could not see me wince at the impact.

I turned around and watched, shocked that their fighting intensified despite this challenge having lasted multiple days without any food.

Was I that strong? Could I handle a fight like that?

Of course, you could, Ares said. He ducked underneath Koda's punch and caught Koda with a sidekick as he darted away.

I growled. *Focus on your fight.*

Our pack had slowly moved closer and closer to me, subconsciously yearning for the nearness of their Alpha female while their Alpha male was engaged in a fight that they could not help him with.

I stretched out and pretended to doze in the warmth of the sun, and they all moved ten feet closer to me, the fear of Ares the only thing keeping them so far from me as it was.

Apollo was among them, but he was the farthest from me, which was smart.

"I submit!" Ares yelled.

I sat upright and growled. What had happened? Why did he submit?

Koda stood over Ares, his claws too close to Ares' throat. "You never could figure out how to counter that attack," Koda said. He plopped to the ground beside Ares and groaned.

"Sneaky," Ares said. He stood up and cleared his throat. "By submission I announce the new Alpha of the Werewolves, Koda."

The pack cheered, everyone except Ares, Koda, and me. Ares walked to me, his body stiff and weariness in his movements. "Let's go to our room," he said.

I stood up and touched my nose to his hand and then teleported us into our room. He collapsed on the bed and sighed. "Thank you. I do not think I could have made it to our room if I had had to walk all the way."

I shifted and then laughed at him. "Of course, you could have. You would not have let the others see such a weakness."

"Are you upset?" he asked me.

I weighed my answer. "I am not sure how to answer your question. Can you be more specific?"

"Are you upset that I submitted?" he asked.

I shook my head and sat on the bed beside him, resting my hand on my handsome mate's face. "No. In fact it feels good knowing that we do not have to rule the werewolves and that the pack is in such good hands."

"You know I submitted on purpose, right?"

I laughed. "Of course, I do. You would not be so easily defeated."

He smiled. "Let's not tell Koda, alright? It's best if he and the rest of the world believe that Koda is the rightful Alpha. I am weary of trying to wrangle you and a thousand werewolves at the same time."

I kissed his cheek and then wrinkled my nose in disgust. "You need a shower."

He rolled on his back, grabbed me, and pulled me down onto my side with my head on his chest. "All I need is you."

I put his hand on my stomach and whispered, "He wants out."

"He?" Ares asked.

I nodded and smiled. "Our son is ready to come out. I suppose that means we should give him a name."

"It's too early for him to come out," Ares said despite the happiness I saw at the news of having a son.

I shrugged. "Victor told me that the baby is ready to come out, and I feel that he is right."

"So, what shall we name him?" Ares asked.

"You can think of names *after* you shower," I said, sitting up and pushing his side.

"Fine," he said, dashing to the bathroom and returning a few minutes later smelling like roses. "Cratus."

"What?" I asked since I had not been paying attention.

He sat down on the bed beside me and spoke in a soft voice as he ran his fingers through my hair. "I would like to name him Cratus."

"Cratus," I repeated, letting the name roll off my tongue so I could try it out. I nodded. "I like it."

Ares smiled. "That was easier than I thought."

"I'm not *always* difficult," I said defensively.

"Only ninety percent of the time," he teased me and then kissed my temple.

Dizziness overwhelmed me, so I gracefully fell onto my side, thankful I was already sitting on the bed.

"Artemis?" Ares asked, concerned at the sudden movement.

"Dizzy," I whispered.

"I'll call Kod—" Ares stopped and laughed. "I guess I can't summon Koda anymore. I'll go get Selene."

I grabbed his hand before he could stand up. "No, don't leave. It'll pass in a moment." The baby started kicking and I groaned at the fierce kicks. "Never mind, get her."

He rested his hand on my stomach, lowered his face until his lips were pressed against my skin and growled, "Calm down, pup."

Surprisingly, the baby listened, and the kicking stopped. "You're amazing," I whispered in awe.

"Let's hope this still works when he is a teenager," Ares said with a laugh.

"What age do you consider a preternatural a teenager?" I asked him curiously. "Humans consider thirteen to nineteen a teenager, but that's not really a teenager for a preternatural."

Ares said, "Trust me. You will know when he is in the teenage years. When he starts rebelling it will be obvious."

"Let's hope he does not tear down an entire civilization during his teenage years like his father," Zeus said as he entered the room.

Ares sighed. "You're never going to let me live that down, are you?"

Zeus frowned at him. "You obliterated an entire civilization. That is not something to easily forget."

"Who are you talking about?" I asked curiously.

Zeus threw his hands up into the air and said, "That's the point! No one even remembers them."

"I was young and angry and stupid," Ares said. "And I will not let my son get so out of control."

"Good luck," Zeus said.

Selene entered the room and asked, "Are you ready, Ares?

We should begin the spell to remove Death's sickness as soon as possible, especially if your child really is going to be born today."

"I need meat and about an hour of sleep and then I will be ready," Ares said.

One of Zeus' servants walked in with a tray piled high with steaks and set it on the table before quickly leaving.

It always interested me how Zeus' servants were so frightened of Ares. Had they seen him at his worst and that was why they were so frightened?

Ares sat at the table and ate his food in silence.

I closed my eyes and then smelled and heard Selene walk over to me. "Are you feeling alright?" she asked.

"I got dizzy for a minute, and then Cratus began kicking and hurting me, but Ares made him calm down."

"Cratus? Him?" Selene asked. "How do you know?"

"I sort of let it slip," Victor said, materializing beside Ares. He looked down at Ares and said, "So, you passed the reins on to your brother?"

"He beat me," Ares said with a shrug. Victor was silent a moment, so I knew Ares was telling him about keeping the fact that he had let him win a secret. Ares resumed eating his steaks and I closed my eyes to rest.

Selene whispered a spell so softly even I could not hear it and then the baby kicked. "Ow," I said. "Don't get him riled up again."

She smiled. "I will try to keep him calm while I check him out." She resumed running her hands along my stomach and then said, "Well, he or she, is in good health, but strangely has grown exponentially. You are right that you could go into labor any time now."

"Okay, everyone out so I can take a nap," Ares said. "If I

don't get some sleep, no one is going to like being around me." I started to get up and he shook his head at me. "Not you. You are staying right here with me."

Zeus and Victor left, whispering conspiratorially to each other and Selene stopped at the door. "I'll be back in two hours to get you for the spell."

Ares nodded and laid down on the bed beside me. He scooted over and draped his arm across my waist, below my bulging belly. "I'm surprised that he grew so quickly without hurting you, but I'm glad too."

"Let's not look a gift horse in the mouth," I said. "Honestly, I don't even know when it happened. I know that while I was searching for Blu with Victor, I felt heavier, but I thought it had something to do with the sickness Death gave you."

"I can't wait to hold him," Ares whispered.

"Will he come out in human form?" I asked.

He nodded and kissed my cheek. "You know we don't change until after we hit puberty."

"Yes, but you and I aren't exactly normal werewolves. Stranger things have happened."

He kissed my cheek again and whispered, "Let's sleep. Soon we will not have time for naps like this."

THE NAP WAS INTERRUPTED before I wanted it to end and no amount of begging kept Ares in bed with me.

Ares left with Selene to perform the spell and I was ordered to stay in bed and as far from the place of the spell as possible. Victor was left to guard me, and I stayed lying on the bed despite knowing how rude it was of me. I wanted to pace or to run out to watch everything, but I could not. I hated being helpless.

Food was brought to me and I sat at the little table in the room and ate it while Victor watched me with a strange expression on his face.

"What?" I finally asked. "Why are you looking at me like that?"

"I'm listening to Cratus," he whispered. "I've never listened to a baby's thoughts before. It's intriguing."

"What's he thinking?" I asked.

"Well, children in general think less with words and more with feelings, especially Cratus since he has not been outside of your womb to see anything yet. He wants to stretch but it's too tight in your stomach."

"He'll be out soon enough," I mumbled.

"Are you going to talk to Koda?" Victor asked.

I grit my teeth and sat up slowly, my belly even larger now. "Eventually."

"He challenged Ares because he injured you. He felt he was defending your honor."

"He is an idiot. Hurting Ares only angers me."

"He wouldn't have hurt—"

"He was going to fight him to the death!" I screamed, interrupting him.

"He would have stopped before that," Victor said. His tone told me that he knew that for certain, which he probably did since he could read thoughts.

"Only after I told him that I would kill him if he killed Ares," I said adamantly. I had meant it, too. Even now, the thought made my blood boil.

"You shocked him when you said that," said Victor with a shake of his head. "You broke his heart."

"Hopefully, he will go find a mate now." It would be good for him to be on his own.

"You'll miss him," Victor said softly.

"Of course, I will, but it's time that Ares and I go off on our own."

"Your mother-in-law is coming," Victor whispered.

I heard her approaching footsteps and then she knocked twice on the door, not waiting for permission before she entered the room and closed the door behind her. She hurried to me and rested her hand on my round belly. "I hadn't believed the rumors, but they are true! How could you have progressed so much so quickly? How are you?"

I smiled at her and patted her hand. "We are fine. I thought you would be with Ares."

She smiled. "He and Selene can handle the spell. Are you ready for labor?"

I dipped my head and admitted, "I'm frightened of the labor."

She patted my hand reassuringly. "It will hurt, but you are strong, and you will do fine."

"Have you heard news about the baby's gender and name?" I asked her. I had wanted to tell her, Zeus, and Hera right away, but we had not had the time.

She narrowed her eyes, and her body stiffened. "You picked a name?"

"You will have a grandson and his name will be Cratus."

"Cratus," she whispered as if trying to recall a memory. She tapped her finger twice and then laughed. "Ares picked the name, didn't he?"

"How'd you know?" I asked, narrowing my eyes suspiciously.

"It was an alter ego of Ares' when he was younger. It's fitting that your halfbreed child inherits it," she answered.

"I had forgotten about that," Victor said.

Cratus kicked hard and then tried to stretch out. I moaned and lay down onto my back to give him more room.

Beatrice rested her hand on my stomach and then looked at Victor. "See how long until the spell is over."

I screamed as my stomach contracted again and again in quick succession.

Beatrice frowned and held my hand. "Your son is coming."

SIXTEEN

VICTOR

I teleported to the Sidhe mound outside the portal where they were performing the spell. Surprisingly, the spell was done, and Ares and Selene were sitting side by side, panting on the ground.

"Did the spell work?" I asked.

They both nodded.

"Then come with me."

Ares and Selene stood stiffly, and Ares asked, "What's wrong?"

I smiled. "Your son is being born."

After teleporting Ares and Selene to Artemis, I teleported to Anabelle, my love. Artemis was adamant about attacking father as soon as she was able to, which meant that I had very little time to say goodbye, and I intended to use all the time I could. I pictured Anabelle's face as I teleported, but arrived as mist to surprise her.

As soon as I arrived, the scent of her blood engulfed me. I materialized and dropped to the ground, taking in the scene before me. Blood covered every wall, piece of furniture, and the floor. The blood was only a couple of days old.

Anabelle lay in pieces across the room, her head motionless on the pillow, a scream stuck on her face. Her beautiful hair was matted with her own blood and stuck to the pillow. I turned towards her mirror to find a message written in her blood. I recognized the writing instantly as my father's.

You can't hide from me, son.

I had kept Anabelle a secret from everyone. She was the first woman I had fallen in love with in my entire life. The first woman whose smile alone could brighten my day.

Now, she was gone. I would never see her smile. I would never hear her laugh. I would never hold her warm body in my arms again.

The emotions I had been holding in broke free.

I screamed in sorrow and anger.

The one woman I had dared to love had been taken from me by my own father. I would kill him for this. I would rip his wretched heart from his body and tear him into pieces like he had done Anabelle, and my heart. And then I would burn every last piece of him.

Two men spoke outside her house and before I had even consciously made the choice, I was outside feasting on their blood. I lifted my blood-soaked face to the sky and screamed.

Tonight, I would feast on every man I saw and tomorrow, I would kill my father.

CHAPTER

SEVENTEEN

ARES

Artemis dozed on the bed, still recovering from the 20-hour labor, two days later.

Cratus was perfect. With my hair and Artemis' purple eyes, he was going to be a ladies' man.

"You're spoiling him," Artemis whispered.

"And I will continue to every day I am with him," I whispered back, rocking the tiny baby in my arms.

Mother walked in and set a tray with a salad, fruits, and meat on Artemis' lap. "Eat every piece," she ordered her.

"Yes, ma'am," Artemis said, and tucked in.

Cratus moved and then started fussing.

"He can't be hungry already," Artemis said with a groan. We had been awake most of the last two days with our incredibly hungry newborn.

"I'll feed him," I offered as I walked to Selene who had already prepared a bottle for him.

Due to Artemis' desire to leave for battle tomorrow, she had opted not to breastfeed. So, the Sidhe had prepared their substitute for breastmilk and were supplying it to us. They had also taught Selene and Artemis how to create some replacement milk magically in case of emergency.

I walked around the room slowly as he ate his bottle and let him hold one of my fingers in his tiny hand. I burped him occasionally, and then when he was done and had fallen asleep, I set him in Artemis' arms so that she could bond with him more.

The instant his skin touched hers, he drew in a deep breath and sighed happily, cuddling up against her. Artemis cradled him to her chest and lay down, cuddling with Cratus as she dozed. She looked so peaceful as she held him, and I felt that peace in me as well.

This was what I wanted after the war was over. As soon as the victory was declared in this war, we would go to one of my properties and bond as a family.

Zeus walked in and hugged me with one arm. "He's going to be a handful."

I smiled and said, "I think I've become used to it with Artemis."

She did not respond which meant she was finally asleep.

"Have you heard from Victor?" Zeus asked quietly as we walked to the other side of the room to avoid waking either of them.

I shook my head. "No. The last time I saw him was when he teleported me here for Cratus' birth two days ago. I thought he was just giving us space."

"No one has seen him in those two days. Not even Dmitri," he said.

That was not like Victor. He had disappeared randomly before, but it was usually just to feed and then he would return in less than half a day's time. Most of those times he took Dmitri with him, though.

Someone knocked softly on the door, and then Theseus poked his head in. "You need to come outside," he whispered to me. I could smell his fear and judging by the whiteness of his skin, he was not accustomed to what he had witnessed.

Mother waved me out, sitting in a chair facing Artemis and Cratus. I could not ask for a better bodyguard than her, so I followed Theseus and Zeus outside of the castle.

The sun was beginning to set, and there, in the center of the grass, sitting on his knees was Victor, covered in blood. I inhaled and was surprised to find that none of the blood on him was his own.

"Victor?" I asked. "Are you alright?"

He looked up at me and the pain in his eyes reminded me of when I had lost Artemis. "Are we ready for battle?" he asked with a lisp due to his fangs extending past his lower lip.

It had been centuries since I'd seen him fail to keep his fangs within his mouth.

"We're leaving tomorrow morning," I said, moving closer to him. I continued to keep my composure because in situations where someone went ballistic, one person needed to remain calm. I had seen him snap before and I had seen him slaughter an entire island of people in minutes. "Artemis needs one more night of rest."

He took a deep breath and stood up, the emotions locked away and his Court face on. "I'll go wash up."

He walked into the castle and I said, "Keep everyone away from his chambers for the next hour. He is composing himself, and if someone bothers him during that time, he could snap again."

Theseus trotted off into the castle obediently.

Zeus asked, "What do you think happened?"

"I have no idea," I whispered. Although I had a feeling that whatever had happened had just ensured our victory over Maurice.

EIGHTEEN

"Waah," Cratus cried, waking me up from my peaceful sleep.

I opened my eyes and kissed his little head where it lay on the bed beside me. "Shh, it's alright, Cratus. Mommy is here." I sat up and Beatrice handed me a bottle to feed him.

"Ares was hungry all the time, like him. I thought he was going to suck me dry," she said with a laugh. "Part of me wished I could have fed him while in my wolf form because that form had three sets of teats to feed him from instead of one pair."

I laughed and cradled Cratus in my arm as I fed him his bottle. "Are you going to watch him while Ares and I go to fight?" I asked her. "I won't feel safe leaving him with anyone, but you." I was extremely thankful for her help since Cratus was born. She had stayed in the room to lend me a hand anytime I asked and had even slept in the chair by my bedside.

"Of course, I will stay and protect him," she said. She looked around and then whispered, "I don't fully trust the

Sidhe still. Part of me is worried that they might try to hurt Cratus while you and Ares are gone."

I didn't say it aloud, but I agreed with her, and sadly felt exactly the same. Even though Hera had seemed to have a change of heart about me after Achilles died, I did not trust the stableness of her emotions, and I did not trust her to be alone with Cratus. They'd already killed one of Ares' children. I wouldn't let them kill another.

"Five more minutes," Ares groaned from the bed beside me.

Beatrice and I rolled our eyes at the same time and she said, "You stop being Alpha for three days and suddenly think you get to sleep in? You're still Beta, you know?"

"I've always been Beta," he said through his pillow. "I'll always be Beta, too. That does not mean that I never get a day to sleep in."

"It is attack day," Victor said. "No one gets to sleep in."

Cratus jumped at the strange voice and spit out his bottle. His little eyes filled with tears as he started crying, and then suddenly stopped. He looked at Victor and then took his bottle back and relaxed against me.

"What was that?" I asked softly, shocked by the sudden rapid changes in his mood.

"Victor used his powers to calm him," Ares said from under his pillow. "I'd appreciate you not doing it again."

"I was simply calming him down since I startled him by my sudden appearance. I would never use my powers on him for anything else," Victor said.

There was something off about Victor. Something different in the way he was acting today. Had something happened?

Ares lifted his head out from under his pillow and lifted a brow at Victor.

Victor smiled and said, "I am fully in control of myself now."

"Are you going to tell me what happened?" Ares asked.

I was right!

Victor sat in the chair beside Beatrice and sighed, "Another time. Let's not get anyone else riled up before we get to the fight."

"The troops are ready," Zeus said as he entered the room.

"Just once, I'd like a room where people didn't pop in unannounced or whenever they wanted," I muttered.

Ares sat up and kissed my cheek. "Soon enough, we will be on our way to our own house where no one but our family of three will be."

"As if you could keep me away," Beatrice said and scoffed with arms folded across her chest, leveling Ares with a challenging glare.

"The dragons have arrived outside the mound," Koda announced as he entered the room. "Artemis, I need you to go greet them." He looked taller and bigger, but I knew he had not grown, and it was simply because he was the Alpha now. Despite still being angry at him, I had to admit he looked good, and being Alpha seemed to suit him.

I gritted my teeth and closed my lips tightly to keep from baring them at him. "I will get dressed and go see them," I said in a clipped tone.

Koda softened and became the friend and packmate I remembered. "Artemis, please don't be mad at me."

I did not answer him and instead, handed Cratus to Ares and walked to the bathroom to get ready.

After the war was over, Koda and I would talk, but until

then I needed to stay away from him, or I would punch him in the face…a few times.

Victor chuckled, and I sighed, knowing I was being childish again.

I braided my hair and got dressed into the battle gear that Hephaestus had made me. I was thankful for being a preternatural and being completely healed and recovered from giving birth already.

Tears built up in my eyes, and I wiped them away quickly. It was harder than I thought to think about leaving Cratus, but I had to do it. I had to end this war and right the balance between all of the races. Beatrice would protect him and take great care of him, and hopefully it would not be too long before I returned and was able to hold him again.

Ares walked inside the bathroom and hugged me. "You don't have to go," he whispered. "You could stay with Cratus here, where it's safe."

I hugged him back and kissed his cheek. "You know I won't do that."

He sighed. "I know, but I had to try." We stayed in the bathroom holding each other for another minute, and then reluctantly separated.

I walked out to Beatrice who was still holding Cratus and took him for one last snuggle. I hugged him tightly and kissed his forehead. "Mommy loves you, Cratus. I'll be back soon."

Cratus looked at me in silence and I felt tears building again. I inhaled his scent, memorizing it and the feel of his baby soft skin, and then handed him back to Beatrice.

"I'll protect him with my life," she said, cradling him against her chest.

I nodded and left the room without another word, afraid that if I said anything else, I would not leave. I grabbed my bow and arrows as I walked out, slinging them over my back.

Koda followed me, but I ignored him and headed to the portal. We walked up the stairs, and I composed myself to face the dragons. My heart still hurt from the loss of Fira, but now was not the time for sadness. Now was the time for fierceness and battle.

I stepped from the portal and found fifty dragons waiting in the field. Stunned, I walked to Blu.

Blu wrapped his long neck around me in a hug, humming softly. "Hatchling, you look well. How is your child?"

"He is beautiful and perfect," I said with a wide smile. "He will stay with his grandmother while we destroy the vampire king."

"Thank you for coming," Koda said. "The werewolves and the alliance appreciate your assistance with this fight."

Blu looked at Koda a moment and then at me. "You are no longer Alpha?"

I shook my head. "Koda is now the Alpha of the Werewolves."

Blu dipped his head to Koda. "I did not know."

"I will go check on everyone else and let you know when we are ready to head out," Koda said. He looked at me a moment, words on his lips and a sad frown on his face, but then he strode back into the portal without a word.

"I did not know you and your packmember had had a falling out," Blu whispered.

"It's nothing worth discussing," I said and waved dismissively. "Did you leave enough dragons to guard the Hive?"

He nodded. "The Hive is well guarded."

"Good. When we arrive at the vampire's castle, I need your dragons to burn and destroy as much of the building as possible. You and I will go to Maurice's chamber and search for the Pegasus egg."

"It may have hatched already," Blu said with a growl. "The demon spawn may already have the baby in his hands."

"Then I shall cut his arms off and take the baby from him."

Blu roared in approval, and the other dragons roared with him.

Ares stepped through the portal but stopped at the sight of the roaring dragons. I held out my hand, and he walked slowly towards me, lifting a brow.

"Everyone is ready," he said once he took my hand.

I hugged him and kissed his lips softly. "Stay safe," I whispered.

He nuzzled behind my ear, and we inhaled each other's scents. "I love you."

I hugged him tighter. "I love you too, Ares."

He pulled back and looked at Blu. "I leave her in your capable claws. Please, keep her safe while we are apart."

Blu bowed his head. "I shall protect her like she is my own."

Ares kissed me again and then stepped into the portal.

It had been incredibly hard to convince him to fight separately, but I had finally won the argument when I had reminded him that he was needed to kill as many vampires as possible. Plus, I would be with Victor, Apollo, and Blu and with the three of them beside me I was sure to survive. I thought of Achilles and cringed. This fight would be different.

Apollo and Victor stepped out of the portal.

Apollo wore armor similar to mine. He smiled and said, "Hephaestus thought it would be fitting if the two of us had matching armor since we're twins."

"It looks good on you," I said with a smile.

"Ready?" Victor asked.

I took a long, deep breath before answering. "Yes."

Apollo took my hand and smiled reassuringly at me. "Let's kill some vampires, Sister."

I nodded, set a hand on Blu to teleport him, and closed my eyes as the other dragons who had the ability to teleport began humming. I opened my eyes after we arrived and found Hera standing at the front of the fight beside Zeus and Ares with the rest of our army behind them.

The dragons took to the skies and Apollo, Victor, and I joined them, circling around the top of our army.

The vampires were standing in formation across the field from our army, fear on their faces despite the fact that they still outnumbered us two to one.

"Tonight, we fight to end the false king's reign," Ares bellowed. "Tonight, we fight for our lost brothers and sisters. We fight to end the slaughter of the humans who cannot protect themselves. When this battle ends, the world will be rebalanced and all shall be equal. Humans, Sidhe, vampires, werewolves, elves, dwarves, ogres, and halfbreeds will all be equal! Kill all who oppose us. Kill them all!"

Our army cheered, screamed, roared, and howled. Then they all flew across the field into the waiting vampires, tearing into them before they were ready to start fighting.

"Now," I screamed.

Blu roared, and twenty of the dragons flew over the field. Starting at the vampires who were not yet engaged by our army, the dragons made a wall of flames that none could escape. They burned the vampires and any who stood with them as they flew towards the castle. In seconds, a third of the vampire army was destroyed. The rest of the dragons, Apollo and I headed to the castle.

The dragons began spitting out fireballs which grew hard as they flew and broke the castle everywhere it landed. Archers began to shoot at the dragons, so Apollo and I broke away, shooting them back with our sun-tipped arrows. Vampires exploded into ash as we shot them, and soon there were no more archers firing upon the dragons.

"There," I shouted as I pointed at the part of the castle where Maurice's chambers were and where Victor was standing on top of the building.

Blu spit a fireball straight at Victor who jumped out of the way. The fireball made the roof collapse, and we dropped into the giant room.

Maurice stood up from his throne and his eyes widened at the sight of Blu. "What are the dragons doing here?" he asked.

"Ensuring the world is returned to its rightful balance," Blu said. "And to watch you die."

Maurice held an egg in his hands.

I growled at him. "Give me back my egg."

He smiled. "This is my dragon egg."

"It's not a dragon," Victor said.

Maurice looked at Victor, noticing him for the first time. "My own son is here to fight against me."

"You killed her, and you thought I would forgive that and come to your side?" Victor asked with a snarl. "You're psychotic."

"You should have never taken that damn halfbreed's side!" Maurice yelled, pointing a finger at me.

"Your reign is over," Victor said. "It is time that I take the throne from you."

"You'll have to kill me first," Maurice hissed.

"I intend to," Victor said with a smile.

I darted forward at the same time as Apollo, as we tried to take the egg from Maurice.

Several vampires poured into the room from the side door and interrupted us. I turned my fingers into claws and began tearing into the vampires, ripping their heads off as I went.

"Back!" Blu shouted.

I grabbed Apollo and teleported back behind Blu as he doused the room in flames, killing all of the vampires who had come inside. Maurice and Victor fought to the right of the room, steering clear of the fire. Victor knocked the egg out of Maurice's hand, and I teleported to him, grabbed the egg, and teleported back to Apollo. "Protect Blu. I'm going to teleport this to the Sidhe realm and then I'll be right back."

Apollo nodded. I teleported to Ares' and my chambers, set the egg down in one of the chairs and smiled at Beatrice. "Guard this, too. It's a gift for Cratus from the dragons."

She nodded, cradling Cratus in her arms. I closed my eyes and teleported back to the battle.

Apollo fought a group of vampire-sidhe who were flying above Blu, trying to shoot him with arrows.

I used my sunlight magic, turning them all to ash.

"Thank you," Blu said and then blew out a jet of flames through the door as vampires began to surge inside.

"You alright?" I asked Apollo.

He nodded, gasping for air. "Just catching my breath."

Victor and Maurice were still battling it out, and it looked like an even match. I wanted to help him in some way but did not want to end up hurting Victor in the process.

What could I do? How could I help him?

"Artemis!" Apollo yelled.

I spun around and ducked just in time to avoid an arrow

aimed at my chest. Apollo returned fire, hitting the vampire with his arrow and turning him to ash.

That had been too close for comfort.

"Apollo, fly up and check on the other dragons," I said.

He obeyed instantly, flying upwards out of the hole in the ceiling.

"Are you okay?" I asked Blu. He nodded, and I flew up and out to the battle where Ares was tearing vampires apart in his half-shift. I flew down to him and joined in the battle.

"You're unhurt," he yelled so I could hear him. "I'm surprised."

"It's still early," I teased him.

He growled in response, and we took a moment to smile at each other before resuming our vampire killing spree.

It seemed strange that these vampires were so easy to kill. Were they all new? Had Maurice turned others just to increase his numbers for battle?

That wouldn't surprise me. He didn't view others as equals, but as pawns for his use.

After a bit, when there were fewer vampires around Ares and me, I teleported to Lyngvi and was happy to see a pile of dead vampires with Koda standing next to them in his half-shift, and children walking around unhurt.

"Everything went well?" I asked him.

He turned and his eyes raked my body, looking for wounds. "Yes. No one was hurt." He walked towards me with shaking hands.

I had mine behind me so he would not see the fists I was making.

"Good," I said.

"How is the battle going?" he asked, stopping a little ways away.

"Still going. I have to get back." I started to teleport, and he grabbed my wrist.

"When are we going to talk?" he asked me, pleading with his eyes.

I turned my head to avoid his eyes and whispered, "I don't know."

"Artemis, I—"

I jerked my hand away and teleported back to Blu.

Was it sad that the battle against the vampires was easier for me than my warring emotions about Koda? Part of me wanted to rip him apart for threatening Ares and for fighting him, while the other part of me wanted to forgive him and go back to being friends, before he told me he loved me, before it had all gone sour.

Blu was still fighting vampires, but he was definitely winning. In fact, he looked bored. I stood next to him and watched Victor and Maurice fight. I could hardly keep track of them.

Victor hit Maurice somehow and it hurt him enough that he stopped and put a hand against his ribs.

"You'll never defeat me!" Maurice screamed at Victor.

Victor ducked under his father's attack and then shoved his hand into his chest, grabbed ahold of his heart, and ripped it out. "You lost the moment you touched Anabelle."

Anabelle? Who was Anabelle?

Maurice's eyes widened and then he fell to the ground.

Victor squatted down and tore apart his father into small pieces . Once finished, he backed away and looked up at Blu. "Would you please torch him to ashes so that I may scoop up the remains and scatter him around the world?"

For someone who had just torn a being apart into tiny pieces, he was rather calm.

Blu exhaled a jet of flame onto the dismembered body until it was all ash.

Victor scooped up the ashes, putting them inside a clear vial, which he then put inside a leather pouch that smelled of sage and rosemary mixed with something faintly smelling like blood. He tied the pouch shut and held it in front of his face. "It was a long reign, Father, but you should have known it would come to this."

Apollo dropped down and said, "The vampires stopped fighting everywhere, even in the locations across the world."

Victor smiled. "The war is over, and a new king has taken the throne." Victor looked at me and said, "You will never have to worry about the vampires again."

It seemed too easy. It seemed like it had ended too quickly to be real.

Victor placed his hand on my shoulder and whispered, "It is over. With your help, I learned to love, and having that love taken away from me prompted my decision to kill Maurice." He kissed my cheek and said, "You are right, there is no reason that every race cannot live together peacefully, and we should remember that we were once humans as well. Come, let's go speak to the world." He took my hand and I flew up into the air and out to the field where the two sets of troops stood facing each other uneasily.

I landed in the center, and Ares rushed out to me. "Are you hurt?" he asked, looking me over.

I took his hand and kissed his cheek. "I'm perfectly fine."

"Selene," Victor called.

She stepped from our battalion and approached Victor. "Yes?"

"Would you mind creating a global broadcast?" he asked.

She took a big breath and then spit into her hand.

Victor cocked an eyebrow and stared at her with an expression of confusion, which made me smile and laugh softly.

Selene drew a square on her hand in the spit and then held her hand up into the air. She chanted a spell I had never been able to master, and a large square appeared in front of Victor. "You may begin," she said.

Victor looked into the square and began his speech. "The world has been living in darkness, overshadowed by the preternaturals' desire to rule over the humans and subjugate them as they had done to us. The former King of the Vampires killed any who opposed him or any who he viewed as a possible threat. That king is dead. I, Victor, am the new King of the Vampires. As king, I vow to work with the Council of Beings to create a world where everyone can live peacefully together, including humans. From this moment on, there will be no more war."

Everyone cheered, throwing their hands up into the air or hugging each other.

Victor cleared his throat, and everyone calmed down again. "Any vampire who attacks another being, unprovoked, will answer to me, and I will not take it lightly. From now on, I own all vampires and you will all listen to me."

"Actually, we own everyone," said a female voice.

All eyes turned to face a woman of immense beauty and power with a man of equal attractiveness and power beside her. She looked out over the crowd until her eyes settled on me. "Hello, Artemis."

Ares appeared at my side and dropped to one knee, bowing to the two. "Greetings, Rhea and Hyperion."

Rhea smiled and the man Ares had called Hyperion folded his arms across his chest.

Rhea said, "Greetings, Son. Rise."

Ares stood and took a small step in front of me, which I hoped the visitors did not understand meant he was trying to protect me from them.

"I see that you were able to save your mate," she said and smiled sweetly.

Ares dipped his head. "Thanks to you, I was."

"She and you are a fitting couple," Hyperion said with an approving nod of his head and relaxed his arms.

"How is the child?" Rhea asked.

"He is doing well," Ares said.

"He," Hyperion said happily. "It is good that you have a male to continue on with your genes. You are a worthy offshoot of me."

"Have you chosen a name?" Rhea asked.

Why were they so interested in us? And what had they meant about owning everyone? What the hell was going on?

"Cratus Lupine," I answered her.

She smiled. "That is a fitting name for a halfbreed baby like him." She turned and looked at Hyperion, who I was beginning to believe was her mate. "Did you bring it with you like I asked?"

He pulled off a bag that had been hanging over his shoulder and opened it. "Of course, I did."

She reached inside and pulled out two beautiful silver rings that gleamed in the sun with strange symbols. "We have come baring gifts to those who are deserving," she said to the crowd. "Artemis Lupine, you and your mate, Ares, have shown true strength, devotion, and unwavering love despite times of trepidation. For your loyalty to the world, and each other, we present you with immunity to silver and absolute immortality." She placed one of the rings on my finger and the other on

Ares' and then whispered, "May your love guide the hearts of others."

My finger burned a moment and then the silver stopped hurting. I looked at Ares.

He asked, "What do you mean absolute immortality?"

Hyperion pulled out a sword and cut off Ares' head. I stared down at the head of my mate and gasped. Seeing his head on the ground confused me enough that I couldn't move to react.

Rhea sighed, "You could have just told him. Why must you be so dramatic?"

"It is better that the world see the truth now so none try to test him," Hyperion said.

Rhea squatted down and picked up Ares' head, placed it on his shoulders, which I realized was even more strange because Ares' body had remained standing. Then, in total awe, we all watched as his neck reattached itself to his body and Ares shuddered and said, "That was unpleasant."

"You get used to it," Hyperion said with a smile as he patted Ares' back.

"You can shift back now," Rhea whispered to me.

I looked down and realized I had taken a half-shift. When had I shifted? I was still in too much shock and it took me a minute to focus enough to shift back to human form.

"Why are you giving so much to them?" Athena growled as she came up. "Why have you forsaken the rest of your children?"

Rhea looked at Athena with the sorrow of a mother whose child had gone astray. "You were given a chance to prove you were different, but you betrayed your daughter for your own selfish needs. Even if your daughter has forgiven you, it does not mean you deserved her forgiveness. Should I give you a gift for treachery?"

Athena stormed away with shame written plainly on her face. I felt bad for her, but in the same token, what had she expected Rhea to say?

Rhea turned to Ares and asked, "Are you sure that you do not want to be King of the Werewolves?"

Ares nodded. "The title rightfully belongs to Koda. I want to raise my pup with my mate without the stipulations of being Alpha."

"None are more dominant than you," Hyperion said and then added, "Except me."

Ares smiled. "Yes, but I am not fit to rule them as I would not put them before my mate or my pup."

Hyperion nodded in understanding.

Rhea said, "Then we have a proposal for you."

Ares tensed beside me, and I held my breath as we waited for her proposal. These beings were very old and anything they offered had to be weighed before an answer could be given.

"We would like you and Artemis to return to our home after your son and daughter are old enough to shift. At that time, we will teach you and your children all that we know, and you will become guardians of this world. Will you accept?"

"We don't have a daughter," I answered right away.

Rhea smirked and said, "Give it a year."

"What does being a guardian of this world entail?" Ares asked and moved closer to me.

"You are a smart boy," Rhea said with a laugh. "Very inquisitive."

"You would be charged with watching and preparing your

children for restoring balance to the world should things get too out of hand," Hyperion said. "I believe you will have a very long time before the balance is shifted again."

"Why didn't you assist us if that is your charge?" I asked, frowning.

Rhea placed her hand on my cheek and whispered, "We have always been with you, child. We created you and protected you from your father and mother, and you flourished into a greater woman than I could have dreamed you would become. Through you, beings who thought they were soulless learned to love. How many can say that?"

I glanced at Victor and he smiled at me, though I could see pain within the pinched corners of his eyes.

"What say you?" Hyperion asked me with a stern expression.

I looked at Ares, and he whispered, "We knew we wouldn't be able to live alone forever anyway."

I laughed and then looked at Hyperion and gave him my most serious face. "We accept."

He smiled and clapped his hands together. The earth shook, causing everyone to wobble as we tried to maintain our balance, and then Hyperion grew taller and taller until he was too big to even fit on the planet. He continued to grow until he looked down at us from outer space and spoke with a voice that boomed. "By the powers as the Father of the Universe, I appoint Artemis Lupine, Ares Lupine, and their children as the Guardians of Peace."

"We accept," Ares and I said at the same time and then gaped at each other since we had not planned on saying anything.

The earth shook again and the tattoo that I had noticed on

Hyperion burned like fire as it was drawn on both Ares' forearm and mine. I growled at the pain but did not cry out.

Hyperion shrunk back down, landing lightly on his feet beside Rhea.

Rhea hugged me and kissed my cheek. "You have turned into a spectacular woman. I am so proud of you," she whispered into my ear.

Tears filled my eyes at the heartfelt approval, and I realized that Rhea was my true mother. Athena and Darren had simply been vessels, which had failed the test Rhea had given them.

"Thank you," I whispered and hugged her back.

She placed a necklace with a red heart around my neck and whispered, "Whenever you want to talk, press the necklace to your chest and Hyperion and I will be able to communicate with you."

I threw my arms around her neck as peace consumed me and I felt fulfilled for the first time.

She patted my back and laughed.

Beatrice cleared her throat and held out Cratus to me. "I figured you wouldn't want to wait another minute, since the battle was over."

I smiled my thanks to Beatrice, took Cratus, and nuzzled his neck, inhaling his scent and realizing that it was all over. Ares and I would be able to raise him in a peace-filled world, and we would be able to do it wherever we wanted without interruption.

Cratus nuzzled his face against mine and then Ares hugged me from the other side of Cratus and rested his face against Cratus' cheek. Cratus exhaled and relaxed between us.

"May I?" Hyperion asked, placing his bag on the ground and extending his hands out towards us.

Ares took Cratus from my arms and handed him to Hyperion without hesitation.

Rhea reached into the bag and grabbed a silver chain necklace and a golden rattle. "For Cratus."

"The necklace is the same as our rings?" I asked.

"Yes." She walked to Cratus and shook the rattle. "May I?"

Ares nodded, and she placed the necklace around Cratus' neck.

Cratus fussed a moment, but Hyperion bounced him in his arms softly and made soft shushing noises. The necklace shortened around his neck so that it was more of a choker than a long necklace like it had been.

Rhea put the rattle in Cratus' hand and showed him how to shake it.

He put the rattle in his mouth and relaxed.

"Why is he developing so quickly?" I asked Ares. "Humans don't develop this fast."

"We aren't human," Ares whispered to me. "He is developing as all preternaturals develop. By tonight he will be crawling and in a couple of days he will be walking."

Rhea turned to Victor and smiled. "You did well, Son of the Darkness. I will take the remains from you."

"Will you dispose of them?" he asked her as he held out the bag.

She nodded, took the bag, and threw it up into the air. It disappeared from our view and she said, "He will burn in the sun's flames."

Hyperion continued to play with the rattle and make cooing noises at Cratus, which dimmed his super tough persona and made me like him even more.

Rhea walked to Hera and Zeus, and considered them with a somber expression. "I cannot bring back your son permanently, but I can bring him back so that you may all say goodbye."

She waved her hands and Achilles appeared in front of Rhea. Hera gasped, but before she could reach him, I ran forward and threw my arms around Achilles' neck.

"I'm sorry," I cried as I hugged him.

He hugged me back and kissed the top of my head. "You have nothing to be sorry for. You and Ares belong together, and I was a fool to think that I could intervene."

"I—"

He put his finger against my mouth and stopped me from talking.

"Where is Apollo?" he asked, scanning the crowd over my head.

Apollo stepped forward, looking afraid and very young despite being over one hundred years old just like I was. "I'm here," Apollo said as he approached.

I stood beside my twin protectively, afraid that Achilles might try to harm him. Achilles looked down at him and said, "I forgive you for killing me, and as Prince of the Sidhe I give you a full pardon for my murder."

Everyone gasped, including me.

"Thank you," Apollo whispered, eyes wide, and then he dropped to his hands and knees with his forehead touching the ground. "Thank you."

"Protect Artemis and Cratus," Achilles whispered. "That is your duty now."

Apollo nodded and stood, putting an arm around my shoulders. "I will."

"Achilles," Hera whispered as tears flowed down her cheeks in a steady stream.

Achilles turned and smiled at his mother. "Mother, I am so

proud of you," he said. She sobbed and he wrapped her up in a tight hug. "I love you."

"I love you, too," she choked out.

Zeus hugged Hera and Achilles at the same time, and then grabbed Ares and pulled him into the hug as well. Achilles and Ares smiled at each other.

Ares said, "I am sorry that I could not save you from Death's hold."

Achilles shook his head. "You were right to save Artemis and your child. I would have done the same thing had I been in your shoes. Can I speak with you privately a moment?" He asked Ares.

Ares nodded and Hera reluctantly released her hold on Achilles. The brothers walked away together, far across the field away from everyone else to talk.

Apollo patted my shoulder reassuringly as he hugged me against his side. "It is good for them both to get some closure," he said.

I knew he was right, but I desperately wanted to know what they were saying. "How relieved are you that you've been officially pardoned?" I asked with a smile.

Apollo whispered, "More than you know. I only hope that in time, the Sidhe learn to forgive me as Achilles did."

I watched Ares and Achilles who were still talking to each other with their arms folded across their chests. Ares nodded briskly a few times as Achilles talked and frowned deeply a few times. They seemed to have finally finished when they hugged each other and headed back towards us.

Achilles stopped at his parents, and Hera hugged him again.

Ares walked to me and Apollo stepped aside so that Ares could put his arm around my shoulders.

"So, what did you two talk about?" I asked.

One side of Ares' mouth quirked up in a smirk. "None of your business."

I sighed, which made him laugh.

Achilles made his rounds, saying goodbye to everyone, but saved me for last. He held my hands in his and smiled at me. "You have grown into an incredible woman," he whispered. "I am glad that I got to see it happen."

My throat was too tight for me to speak and tears were threatening to break free at any moment, but I forced my lips to move. "I will never forget you. I will tell my children about you and your brave sacrifice. Everyone will know what a great warrior you were and how wonderful you were."

He bent down and whispered into my ear, "I will always love you and watch over you, and I will always be in your heart. Do not let your relationships with others fail as I had with Ares. *Verus amor vincit omnia.* I love you." His lips touched my cheek in a gentle kiss and then he was gone.

I wanted to scream at Rhea and make her bring him back, but I bit my tongue and walked to Zeus who pulled me into a tight hug, letting me bury my face into his chest as tears escaped, despite my greatest efforts to hold them in.

"Now is the time for rebuilding and peace," Rhea called out. "Any who oppose this peace shall answer to us. Let the Earth unite as one world instead of different nations. You may all be different beings with different backgrounds, but you are all children of the All-mother, Gaia."

People cheered all around me. I took a deep breath, shoved my feelings down, and turned away from Zeus, walked to Ares and took my place by his side. Cratus squirmed in his arms and I took him, cradling the baby against my chest and kissing his forehead.

Even though in the end I had hardly raised a finger in the final battle, it was finally over. Ares and I could finally build a house and raise our child and live as a normal family should. Despite the pain I had experienced over the years and the pain Ares had endured, it was all worth it to finally have our happily ever after.

Ares kissed Cratus' head and then kissed my lips softly. "So, where are we going to build our house?" he asked as people crowded around Rhea and Hyperion for a chance to meet them.

I smiled and grabbed his hand. "I believe your meadow is the perfect place, don't you?"

"I was hoping you would say that."

I lifted our clasped hands and kissed the back of his hand as I pictured the meadow where flowers were blooming, bees were buzzing, and animals ripe for hunting awaited us. "Let's go home."

EPILOGUE

Immediately following the battle, the Council of Beings was created and each group was given a headquarters where the leaders were to live. However, everyone else was instructed to live together and that we were not to section ourselves off anymore. Areas like Las Vegas, Rome, and Paris were rebuilt, and millions moved together, opening businesses and helping each other.

Victor made a lot of changes within the vampire community and despite his battles, he still had a long way to go. It was hard to change people who had been set in their ways for hundreds of years, but with Dmitri's help, he was making headway. I only hoped that they both might find love again so that the sad looks they had when looking at Ares and I together would leave.

I made up with Koda, deciding that I should take Achilles' words of wisdom and not lose a friendship like ours. Despite being very powerful and being known around the world for his skills, he was challenged to fight many battles. However, he won all of them easily and even found a mate who was just as quirky as he was. Anastasia was standing on the sidelines during one of his fights and the sight of her pierced nose, lips, and eyebrow, and half shaved head caught his attention. He flirted with her during his fight and in the end, convinced her to go out with him. The two had been inseparable ever since.

Ares took Apollo under his wing and was teaching him everything he knew. I worried at first that he might snap one day and hurt him, but it seemed that due to Achilles forgiving Apollo and whatever Achilles had said to Ares, that he forgave Apollo as well. We built a house for Apollo a few miles away from ours, and together they trained every single day. Cratus watched and listened, and I had no doubts that he was learning just as Apollo was.

Beatrice built her own house deep within the forest, about ten miles from ours, but visited Cratus every day and took him and Apollo on hunting trips with her. She was taking her role as Grandmother like a full-time job, which was nice because it gave Ares and me time alone.

Cratus loves Blu, and we visited the hive at least once a month. Cratus' powers and skills have developed much faster than I thought they would, and his magic was even more powerful than a child his age should have been. With the Council's help, we were helping him understand how to control his emotions and his powers, but even the Council was shocked with his quick growth. He is a sweet boy though, and I had no doubt that he would become one of the greatest leaders in the world when he was older and might even surpass Ares in power.

Our daughter, Solara, was born exactly a year from the day Rhea had told us. She takes after her father when it comes to anger, but her powers were primarily sun based. She loved creating little balls of sunlight at night to dance with fireflies.

I loved seeing my two children playing together and with our other children in the pack.

The number of halfbreeds increased quite a bit and I knew the population would continue to grow now that Maurice and his evilness was gone.

The world is far from perfect, but the fear is slowly evaporating, and people are smiling a little more every day. Every type of being can be seen working and living side by side and even though we know the peace won't last forever, we are enjoying it while we can. Together we were stronger than ever and together we could accomplish anything.

THANK YOU

Thank you for reading the Artemis Lupine Series. This was the first series I ever wrote and published and holds a special place in my heart. Knowing that you took the time to read the full series makes me happier than you will ever know.

If you enjoyed it, please consider leaving a review.

CONNECT WITH CATHERINE BANKS

I really appreciate you reading my book! I hope you enjoyed it.

Please consider leaving a review at your favorite site.

Here are some ways to connect with me:

www.catherinebanks.com

Follow me on BookBub: https://www.bookbub.com/authors/catherine-banks

Join my Patreon: http://www.patreon.com/catherinebanks

Purchase items handmade by Catherine: http://Etsy.com/shop/TurboKittenInd

About the Author

Catherine Banks is a USA Today bestselling fantasy author who writes in several fantasy subgenres and has multiple pseudonyms. She began writing fiction at only four years old and finished her first full-length novel at the age of fifteen. She is married to her soulmate and best friend, Avery, who she has two amazing children with. After her full-time job, she reads books, plays video games, and watches anime shows and movies with her family to relax. Although she has lived in Northern California her entire life, she dreams of traveling around the world. Catherine is also C.E.O. of Turbo Kitten Industries™, a company with many hats including being a book publisher and Etsy store full of nerdy fun.

facebook.com/catherinebanksauthor
twitter.com/catherineebanks
amazon.com/author/catherinebanks
bookbub.com/authors/catherine-banks

MORE FROM CATHERINE BANKS

<u>**YOUNG ADULT PARANORMAL & FANTASY ROMANCE SERIES**</u>

<u>***Artemis Lupine Series***</u>

Song of the Moon

Kiss of a Star

Healed by the Fire

Battles of the Night

Artemis Lupine, The Complete Series

<u>***Little Death Bringer Duology***</u>

Mercenary

Protector

Little Death Bringer, The Official Coloring Book

<u>***Pirate Princess Series***</u>

Pirate Princess

Princess Triumvirate

ADULT PARANORMAL & FANTASY
ROMANCE SERIES

Zodiac Shifters Paranormal Romance Series
Centaur's Prize
Tiger Tears
Lion About

Ciara Steele Novella Series
True Faces
Barbaric Tendencies

ADULT REVERSE HAREM PARANORMAL & FANTASY
ROMANCE SERIES

Her Royal Harem Series
Royally Entangled
Royally Exposed
Royally Elected
Royally Enraged
Her Royal Harem, The Complete Series
The Demon's Fair
Her Royal Harem, The Coloring Book

Wings of Vengeance Series
Of Dragons and Cruelty
Of Minotaurs and Sacrifice
Wings of Vengeance, The Complete Series

Anderelle: Minloa Trilogy
Queen of the Stars
Empress of the Galaxy
Goddess of the Universe
Anderelle: Minloa, The Complete Series

Bonds of Madness Series
Sealing the Deal
Racing the Clock

Her Super Harem Series
Lucky Strike

Her Hellish Harem Duet
A Demon's Heart
A Demon's Soul*

*Coming Soon

MORE FROM CATHERINE BANKS

STANDALONE YOUNG ADULT PARANORMAL & FANTASY ROMANCE BOOKS

Monster Academy

Daughter of Lions

Lady Serra and the Draconian

Of Sky and Sea

The Last Werewolf

Sybil Deceived

STANDALONE YOUNG ADULT PARANORMAL & FANTASY REVERSE HAREM ROMANCE BOOKS

Moon Academy

STANDALONE ADULT PARANORMAL & FANTASY ROMANCE BOOKS

Demonic Contract

Anja's Secret

Dragon's Blood

Last Ama Princess

Transforming Rose
Alys of Asgard
Phoenix Possessed
Stone Heart

STANDALONE URBAN FANTASY BOOKS
The Pawn

CHILDREN'S BOOKS
Calvin's Alien Adventure

MORE FROM DAISY EMORY

The Boyfriend Deal

Their Purple Girl

ACCIDENTAL MOBSTER SERIES
Accidental Mobster
Unintentional Pirate
Suddenly Baroness*

*Coming Soon